"You may be right," he said, putting one arm across the top of the booth back, looking more relaxed than she'd ever seen him. "You certainly seem to enjoy *your* favorite hobby."

"Which would be?"

"Provoking me."

On the brink of denial, Eden felt her own laughter bubble up. "I have devoted a lot of time to that lately, haven't I?" It was a surprisingly nice sensation—the firelight, the food and this odd coziness with Gideon, of all people.

Aware that he'd been feeding her this entire time and neglecting his own meal, she dipped a mac-and-cheese ball in the chili sauce, set it on an appetizer plate and slid the dish toward him, licking sauce off her thumb.

"So," she said, crossing her arms and leaning on the table, her smile easy and genuine as she enjoyed the gentle epiphany of connection. "Should we be friends now?"

Dear Reader,

Holidays can be complicated. Whose house do we go to for Thanksgiving? Will the holidays be stressful or joyous or both? Do we greet each other with happy holidays? Merry Christmas? Hanukkah *sameach*? *Heri za* Kwanzaa? In Holliday, Oregon, anything goes, because every holiday is celebrated and shared—together, as a community.

For *Moonlight, Menorahs and Mistletoe*, the focus is on Hanukkah, a holiday aglow with candles, vibrant with music and dreidels and people frying up platters of latkes or *sufganiyot* (jelly doughnuts—yum!). Usually there's a retelling of the story of King Antiochus's attempt to abolish Judaism and the Maccabees' victory over his army against all odds. We celebrate the miracle that one small jar of oil, enough to provide just twenty-four hours' worth of flame, lasted eight nights. But it's more than that.

The light-filled holiday reminds us to appreciate and protect our uniqueness—other people's, as well—and never to allow a tyrant of any size to minimize or homogenize or erase us. Sometimes that tyrant is our own fear. Especially the fear of letting someone see who we really are.

For a long time now, both Eden Berman and Gideon Bowen have been afraid to live fully or love passionately. There are mistakes too difficult to overcome and risks too terrifying to take. At least, that's what they've told themselves. But in a town like Holliday, in a season where wonders abound, they're about to discover that anything is possible.

Thank you for visiting Holliday! I hope you'll return soon for Nikki's story, the next book in the series.

May your celebrations be filled with the magic of love.

Wendy

Moonlight, Menorahs and Mistletoe

WENDY WARREN

HARLEQUIN
SPECIAL
EDITION

HARLEQUIN®
SPECIAL EDITION™

Recycling programs for this product may not exist in your area.

ISBN-13: 978-1-335-40826-6

Moonlight, Menorahs and Mistletoe

Copyright © 2021 by Wendy Warren

This edition published by arrangement with Harlequin Books S.A.

For questions and comments about the quality of this book, please contact us at CustomerService@Harlequin.com.

Harlequin Enterprises ULC
22 Adelaide St. West, 40th Floor
Toronto, Ontario M5H 4E3, Canada
www.Harlequin.com

Printed in U.S.A.

Wendy Warren loves to write about ordinary people who find extraordinary love. Laughter, family and close-knit communities figure prominently, too. Her books have won two Romance Writers of America RITA® Awards and have been nominated for numerous others. She lives in the Pacific Northwest with human and nonhuman critters who don't read nearly as much as she'd like, but they sure do make her laugh and feel loved.

Books by Wendy Warren

Harlequin Special Edition

The Men of Thunder Ridge

Do You Take This Baby?
Kiss Me, Sheriff!
His Surprise Son

Home Sweet Honeyford

Caleb's Bride
Something Unexpected
The Cowboy's Convenient Bride
Once More, At Midnight

Logan's Legacy Revisited

The Baby Bargain

Family Business

The Boss and Miss Baxter
Undercover Nanny
Making Babies
Dakota Bride

Visit the Author Profile page
at Harlequin.com for more titles.

For the rebbes,
including Reverend Dave Richardson,
who told me, "Explore Judaism."

Chapter One

Holliday, Oregon, was at its most beautiful in the fall. Vine maples as richly red as the local pinot noirs, the licking orange and gold flames of oak and birch leaves turning as autumn burst across the Willamette Valley in all its customary unsubtle glory.

In contrast to the explosive color, the wind whispered on this November morning, its breath chilly but still a week or so away from the puff-cheeked blow of true winter. And inside Holliday House, a three-story, brick Federal-style building that housed the local history museum, information center, a small library and a popular tea room,

Eden Berman sat at her desk, warm and comfortable, yet tingling with anticipation.

Back straight, arms at ergonomically correct ninety-degree angles and fingers poised above the keyboard, Eden scanned the area immediately around her to make absolutely certain she was audience-free. No way did she want anyone to see what she was typing.

The only patron in this morning was Sherry Rhoades, recently elected president of the Holliday Historical Society, who lounged near the reference section of the museum's small library, ostensibly perusing a copy of *Pictorial History of the Willamette Valley*. Eden knew the woman had tucked a copy of *Fifty Shades Freed* inside the history book's cover. Sherry would be ungainfully occupied for the next hour, at least. There was no one else close by, so…

With adrenaline pumping in her veins, Eden tapped the keys as quietly as possible.

Brandon Buchanan.

Mrs. Brandon Buchanan.

Eden Berman Buchanan. Ooh, didn't *that* one have a nice ring to it?

Brandon and Eden Buchanan.

Brandon Buchanan and the former Eden Berman…

Each letter that popped onto the screen made her feel fizzy, as if she'd taken a sip of champagne.

She could totally picture the *chuppah*—birch poles, wild similax and roses!—and Brandon stomping on a glass to cries of *"Mazel Tov!"* He wasn't Jewish, but they would honor each others' traditions.

Not that she was engaged yet, or even dating. Nosiree, she was as single as she'd been when she'd moved to Holliday a decade ago. And until just recently, she had preferred it that way.

She was thirty(ish), financially independent, lived in a very nice one-bedroom apartment with built-in bookshelves and engineered hardwoods, and she had a cat. Nothing too shabby about that picture. Although the cat hadn't been her idea. It had simply appeared on her patio one evening around dinnertime, cranky and hungry-looking, and when she'd tried to ignore it (because you're not supposed to feed someone else's cat, right?), it had hurled itself repeatedly against the sliding glass door.

Eden had opened the slider a crack—just a crack—to tell it to go on home and get a Xanax, but it had streaked past her, jumped onto the coffee table and devoured her pad thai. The freeloader had been eating her out of house and home, not to mention waking her up to play at 2:00 a.m., ever since.

Nevertheless, Eden had thought her life was pretty good. No need to make any major adjustments...

until two things happened. First, her closest friend, Nikki, and then her brother, Ryan, had both met their life partners and were now planning weddings. That wouldn't have thrown her ordinarily. She'd caught that illness once herself and barely made it out alive. Considering herself immune for life, she'd said a quick prayer for her friend, her bro and their future spouses, then planned engagement parties and showers and attended numerous wedding dress hunts and cake tastings. In her own life, she'd carried on as usual, expecting not much to change, but then she'd begun to feel…different. Off-kilter. Restless and itchy, as if it was the hottest part of summer, and she was stuck in a wool sweater she couldn't take off. That's when the second thing happened—

Brandon Buchanan moved to Holliday.

With another furtive glance at Sherry, Eden kicked off the leopard-print stilettos that were pinching her toes and tapped the keyboard again, switching to a screen shot of a photo that had appeared in the local paper a month ago. In it, Brandon Angus Buchanan, who was 100 percent Scots on both sides (*Outlander*, anyone?), stood grinning in the middle of a group of local youth. The man was six foot two if he was an inch and appeared capable of hoisting a minivan with two-point-four kids and a Labradoodle onto his broad shoulders after participating in a Highland Games log toss.

His face, on the other hand, was reassuringly

average. Nose a *little* too large, lips on the thin side, eyes sincere and crinkly around the corners when he smiled. Wasn't that wonderful? Brandon Buchanan was just an average guy who looked as if he could keep a woman's heart safe and warm her entire life.

To be clear, it wasn't his looks that made her blood rush. (That was a lie; his looks made her blood pump plenty!) But they weren't the *only* thing that impressed her. Brandon was a good guy. No—Brandon was a mensch. Despite moving to town just last spring, the man had already coached a peewee soccer camp, started a social action group for youth that he called "Community Kids" and taught Danny Ziddle, who had Down syndrome, how to catch a baseball so he could sit on the bench with the rest of the boys instead of merely being in charge of snack distribution like he'd been doing year after year just to feel included.

Brandon had been hired to teach history at South Willamette High beginning this fall. (All that and a master's degree, too!) Phone calls and emails had been pouring into beleaguered Principal Casey's office as parents—mostly mothers— requested Mr. Buchanan for their students.

How had Eden come by all this information about a man with whom she had yet to trade a single word? Simple. Holliday, Oregon, was a small town, or small enough. The museum-slash-info-center-slash-library-slash-tearoom where she'd worked for years now was not only a tourist destination, but also the hub of local committee meetings and book clubs and gossip sessions. She heard stuff.

Holliday had a total population of 7,453, of whom Brandon was resident number 7,452. He'd arrived solo—no wife, no girlfriend, not even a sofa until he'd brought the Statlers' "like new" sectional at the neighborhood-wide yard sale.

Ergo, Brandon Angus Buchanan, burgeoning pillar of the community, was quite likely up for grabs.

Eden's fingers danced across the keyboard again.

Eden Lea Berman and Brandon Angus Buchanan, together with their parents, request the pleasure of your company at their wed—

"Good morning, Ms. Berman. Or it would have been if I'd had any sleep last night."

Gah! Dang it. The voice, a cross between Scotty McCreery and Darth Vader, startled her so badly she typed *weddingurgurk*. As swiftly as she could, Eden switched to a spreadsheet titled Community Hanukkah Volunteer Schedule so Gideon Bowen, Harbinger of Doom, would not see what she'd been writing.

"For Pete's sake, where did *you* come from?"

she snapped, forgetting to use her welcome-to-your-local-museum manners.

"My office," Gideon answered, lowered brow and wavy hair as black as his soul.

Sheesh, lighten up, Cruella, her conscience admonished. *Dude can't be* that *heinous.*

Alas, her conscience was wrong. Dude *was* that heinous, and Eden was not the only person in town who thought so.

Gideon was Holliday, Oregon, resident number 7,453, having acquired dear old Doc Shlessinger's family medical practice three months ago. Most folks said they couldn't understand what the long-time physician had been thinking when he'd sold to Gideon. Before he'd retired, Doc S. had still made house calls. He'd accepted meat loaf and a pan of seven-layer bars as payment when Lynnette Murphy and her husband lost their insurance, and he'd held an open house once a year, with a barbecue, a bouncy house for the kids and a photo booth. It was practically tradition for the local doctor to be a sweetheart. The town's biggest park was named after the former local physician and philanthropist. But Dr. Bowen?

Requests for house calls were now referred to the urgent care clinic in Albany, and he couldn't be bothered with the open house. Janette Timmons, his receptionist, had offered to get the ball rolling since he was new in town, and you know what he told her? "I'm not a party person, Ms. Timmons."

Just like that. No discussion, no concern for local tradition. It was safe to say Gideon would not be getting a park named in his honor anytime soon. No one knew much about him, but more than a few people had come to Eden hoping for enlightenment, or a bit of gossip as grist for the mill. Why her? Because Gideon wasn't only the town doctor; he was also her new landlord.

"What are you doing here?" she asked, company tone still on hold.

"Looking for information. The sign outside says Information Center, and you're the person to speak with, correct? Unless your button is strictly ornamental."

Positioned between her shoulder and bosom, the button proclaimed, Ask Me Anything… Within Reason. She'd pinned it onto a fitted, 1950s vintage dress with a keyhole bodice. Very sexy. She'd been channeling Ava Gardner lately and had even dyed her naturally auburn hair a deep mink brown.

"Nothing about me is strictly ornamental, Dr. Bowen." She batted her mascaraed lashes. "What kind of information do you require?"

The man hadn't even glanced at her chest, which was widely acknowledged to be her best feature and shown to advantage in the keyhole dress. He'd never spared her more than a passing glance, ever, unless he was irritated about something, which was most of the time, and then he looked sinister.

"Has anyone ever mentioned that you bear a striking resemblance to Voldemort?" she asked pleasantly.

His expression did not budge from aloof indifference. "Only my mother, but she promised I'd outgrow it."

Eden shook her head. "Wait… Did *you* just make a *joke*?"

"I don't think so. I have no sense of humor."

And in fact his face remained completely impassive. Interestingly, it wasn't a bad face. Eden rested her chin on her palm. "You know, if you ever smiled, you could look handsome."

Well, what do you know? A brief…something… skittered across his features. A definite change in expression, though it was just a flash and quickly disappeared. "On the other hand," she mused, "you might look like you've just eaten an angel." She nodded as if giving this great thought. "Yeah, better not smile."

His well-shaped lips did something, twitched a bit. And deep inside the eyes that were so dark gray it was hard to distinguish iris from pupil, there was some flicker of emotion that, for once, did not look like irritation.

She had to admit that when she wasn't irked

by her new landlord and neighbor—he occupied the larger owner's unit in the duplex she rented—Eden found him to be a somewhat interesting puzzle. She judged Gideon to be an inch or two over six feet. He had beautiful posture—had to give him that—and thick, wavy black hair that was cut short. Life had etched lines around his mouth—prematurely, she guessed. Quite likely he wasn't beyond his late thirties, but his demeanor made him seem older. From the first time they'd met—the day he'd introduced himself as her landlord—she'd thought he looked like someone with a story to tell, one with unhappy bits she'd be able to relate to, and she'd felt a stimulating curiosity. Because they lived next door, sharing a common bedroom wall, in fact, she'd imagined that their landlord-rentee relationship might blossom into a comfortable buddy thing, the kind in which one of them could knock on the wall, and the other would know the knock meant, "*The Crown* is starting. Bring popcorn and Flake bars."

Then he'd spoken to her and ruined everything.

"I'm Dr. Bowen. I've purchased this duplex. I don't know what the previous policy was on parties, but I prefer that you not have any. You're welcome to entertain a reasonable number of guests on your patio between the hours of nine a.m. and ten p.m. Before or after, I would appreciate your

keeping the noise inside and the decibel level to a minimum..." And on and on it had gone.

Looking for a guy who knows how to have a good time? Swipe left.

Eden had listened to him with her jaw slack. Who said stuff like that? She...*they*...lived in a duplex in a neighborhood that made Mayberry look like Miami by comparison. What exactly did he think she was going to do on her patio?

"No fun before nine or after ten. Gotcha," she'd agreed, cocking her finger at him.

"If it's easier for you, I can provide a hard copy of the guidelines," he'd offered, dead serious.

She'd set her lips in an extra wide smile. *"No thanks. I'm pretty sure I couldn't forget this moment if I tried."*

At the end of their meeting, she'd closed her door, considered hiring movers, then phoned a few friends instead, inviting them to her place that night for a rousing game of Pictionary. On the patio. With strings of glowing twinkle lights, a fire pit and music. Loud music.

Immature? Unquestionably. Petty? Mmm... yeah, okay. It wasn't like her to react with malice aforethought, but she'd wanted him to get the message loud and clear: *You're not the boss of me.*

A sealed envelope containing a typed hard copy of Gideon's house rules had been left in her mailbox the next day.

"So what kind of information are you looking for?" she repeated her question now, gazing up at him.

"Pet care."

"Pet care? You have a pet?"

"No, you do. And I suggest you learn how to take care of it."

Oh, drat.

"Would you like me to elaborate?"

"No, I'm good."

"Your cat began yowling outside my bedroom window at two a.m. It continued to yowl until three this morning."

Ouch. Dang cat. Eden was about to apologize— really—when he continued.

"If you're going to have a pet, please be responsible for it. I get up at four every morning. I never got back to sleep, which means I am working on only three hours of rest today."

"You get up at four? And you don't go to bed until—" she did the mental math…awakened at two, had only three hours of sleep… "—eleven? So typically you sleep five hours? How do you survive?" This bit of information made him more interesting to her. "Four a.m., sheesh. Might as well be a bat. I'd get up at noon if I could get away with it. Later if I had a really good reason to stay in and snuggle." She gave him her best naughty-girl eyebrow wriggle.

Gideon did not respond; he merely gazed at her with his inscrutable Mount Rushmore expression. Crossing her arms, she leaned back in her chair. "So, why do you try to operate on too little sleep? Holdover from your med-student days? You know, since Doc Shlessinger's office doesn't open until eight thirty, you could stay under the covers until seven and still be squeaky clean and caffeinated in time for work."

Placing his palms on her blotter, Gideon leaned his tall body over her desk. "Ms. Berman, listen to me. Please." He spoke with exaggerated patience, but for once he sounded less like he was issuing a command and more like he was explaining. "I don't want to stay under the covers until seven. I want to sleep—uninterrupted—when I'm in bed. Can you appreciate that?"

"Not really." That wasn't what she wanted *at all*. Popping quickly to mind was the image of Brandon Buchanan, pajama bottoms in the colors of his clan tartan slung low on his hips, his sculpted chest bare and a dreamy smile on his full lips as he woke her from sleep, because he couldn't get enough of the two of them together. They'd make love at two in the morning—never mind work the next day; raid the kitchen for chocolate-covered graham crackers and peanut butter cup ice cream, because they both agreed that was the best combination on the planet; then snuggle under the covers, constructing ice cream sandwiches while they discussed all the news on Yahoo until they were bleary-eyed and fell asleep in each other's arms.

"You think this is amusing?" Gideon's deep voice popped a tiny hole in her happy bubble.

"Hmm?"

"You're grinning." Straightening, he shoved a hand through his hair, making the waves unruly, which looked better on him. "This is futile," he muttered, shaking his head. "For people like you, everything's a joke."

Surprise made Eden uncross her arms and sit up. "People like me? What does that mean?"

A long, gimlet-eyed pause preceded his flat pronouncement, "People your age, for one thing. You seem to think being frivolous is an attribute. Life's still just a game."

The seedlings of anger had Eden rising from her chair. She faced Gideon squarely. "Wait just a minute, buster. You don't know me or what I was thinking. In the first place, I was not smiling about *you*. I was smiling because—" *Ooh. Nope, not goin' there.* "Listen, frivolous is one thing I am not. Besides…'people my age'? C'mon, I'm thirty-six!" Her voice rang loudly in the still-quiet foyer. Sherry Rhodes's head jerked up, and Eden quickly recanted. "I *will be* thirty-six. In a few years." She smiled brightly at Sherry. Lowering her voice, she looked at Gideon and promised, "I was not being frivolous just now." Pointing discreetly in Sherry's direction, she mouthed, *"Huge gossip."* Which, she realized, still made her look frivolous, because why should she care if Sherry told everyone she was thirty-six when it was the truth? Except that Brandon Buchanan was only thirty-one, and Eden already had a few insecurities…well, one big one… about her ability to attract the man. Her most recent birthday didn't help matters.

"Would you like a cup of tea?" she asked Gideon very nicely, exerting the effort to change tack. They'd gotten off on the wrong foot—a couple of times—but they could turn things around. After all, she never made enemies. Ever. She was gracious and entertaining, and she practiced tolerance toward everyone (except him).

Gesturing to the tearoom, where lead server Sandy Linstrom was writing the specials on a chalkboard, Eden offered, "We'd love for you to be our guest this morning. Holliday House Tea Room and Café has several green, black and herbal blends—"

"I don't want tea."

"—plus a variety of yummy breakfast treats."

"I don't want breakfast."

"Our lunches are quite popular, too. I recommend the wild mushroom quiche if you'd like to come back around noon."

"No."

"Fine. How about a snack item to stave off low blood sugar, which can make a person cranky?"

Beneath a white lab coat with a pen clipped to the breast pocket, Gideon's chest rose and fell sharply. "I don't want anything to eat. Or drink. All I want is a tenant who can follow simple, clear guidelines intended to make living next door to each other a reasonably positive experience."

"'Reasonably positive.' Aiming awfully high there, aren't you, homeboy?"

Gideon's face was all angles and shadows as he gazed at her. She wished she could tell what he was thinking. Or maybe not. His eyebrows lowered by increments until they looked as if they were going to obscure his vision.

Strong jawline, high cheekbones, thin nose in addition to skin that was too pale for his dark hair reminded Eden of Edward in *Twilight*. Maybe Gideon was the undead.

Or just undernourished. Beneath the lab coat, his stomach was almost too flat.

Felipa Ramos, who owned Thanksgiving, the local diner, reported that Gideon stopped in for takeout a few times a week. He never got the same thing twice (an adventurous eater at any rate), but neither Felipa nor any of the other restaurant owners in town had seen him request a table. She'd eaten alone quite a bit, too, when she'd first moved to Holliday. No matter how much she'd told herself independence was invigorating, there'd been a gnawing loneliness.

A surge of sympathy—even if she was merely projecting—softened Eden's attitude, propelling her to offer the apology she owed him.

"About the cat," she said, "it's not *really* mine, but I'll try to keep it—"

She was talking to Gideon's back. Somewhere between "About" and "mine," he turned and walked toward the front door.

"Um, so should we keep working on the whole reasonably positive neighbor thingy?" she called after him. Swinging open the door, he headed onto Liberty, the main street running through town. "Okay. Thanks for dropping by."

Eden watched him walk past the window, white coat flapping, without a backward glance for the museum or its curator, presumably on his way back to work.

Opening her desk drawer, she pulled out her smartphone, texted herself the note Check local listings for rentals with three exclamation points, then replaced the phone and shoved the drawer shut. She loved her little apartment, but how enjoyable was it going to be to live next door to a man who made a recluse spider seem chummy?

Maybe Gideon Bowen was her crossroads, the motivation to change things up, kick her life into high gear. She'd lived in the same place since moving to Holliday. Twelve years ago, a space that accommodated only one person had seemed like a good fit, because she'd been certain at the tender age of twenty-four that marriage, or even cohabitation, was off the table.

Switching back to the screen with the photo of Brandon surrounded by his group of "Community Kids," she waited for the pang of hunger she'd been feeling lately, and, yep, there it was, but not in her stomach. This was a hunger deep and achy in the center of her chest.

She wanted more. More than the perfectly fine life she had right now.

Twelve years ago, she'd lost the courage to hope for what other women her age took for granted: that someday they would find a strong, enduring love. She'd become afraid to want anything average, like a loving family of her own, because she wasn't. Average. Hadn't been for so long that, honestly, she'd already forgotten what it felt like.

Now at thirtyish—thirty-sixish—she wondered if maybe, just maybe there was a man out there who would take her as she was. A man whose mind and heart were so big there would be room for her and her assorted baggage.

Anticipation fluttered in her belly as she clicked one last time (honest) on the photo of Brandon standing proudly with an arm draped around Danny Ziddle's shoulder. Just last week Danny had told his mother, who volunteered two hours a week at the museum, that Brandon gave him "jobs to do, like the other kids!" In the photo, Danny's smile was almost bigger than his face. *"I think Brandon makes him feel like one of the guys,"* his grateful mother, Beth, had confided.

Maybe Eden was never going to feel like one of the "in" people, like someone who never had to worry about being accepted or valued exactly as she was, but for the first time in forever she thought she might be able to love again. If she felt safe…if the odds were pretty good that she could trust someone completely…then maybe her life story wouldn't have the super-blah ending she sometimes feared. It would take a special man.

"You're it, Brandon Buchanan," she whispered under her breath, feeling her heart skitter like water on a hot skillet. "Please don't disappoint me."

Chapter Two

Shuffling the toes of her T-strap pumps through the tufts of leaves already on the ground, Eden mused that walking through town on a late fall evening was hands down one of her favorite activities in Holliday. It wasn't quite cold enough yet for a down jacket, but curls of fragrant wood smoke rose from several chimneys. And judging from the scent of cinnamon wafting through every street, the Holliday Fruit & Nut Company was baking the apple pies that regularly drew customers from Portland, Salem and beyond. With Thanksgiving around the corner and Hanukkah only a couple of days after that, the town would soon be scented with treats of all kinds.

Eden had stopped at her apartment after work to change clothes and collect the flowers and dessert she was bringing to Barney and Charlene Gleason's weekly Friday night gathering. Gideon hadn't been home yet, which had saved her the trouble of either seeing him or, more accurately, trying to avoid him. After explaining to the cat that he would have to remain quietly indoors until further notice, she changed his litter box, set out his nightly buffet, loaded *The Secret Life of Pets* on Netflix and pressed Play before she set off.

There was a definite bite in the air, which had prompted her to don her long red box coat. Behind her, a rolling wagon squeaked companionably, bouncing over cracks in the sidewalk as she approached the Gleasons' two-story bungalow.

"What do you have there?" Barney called out as she arrived, descending his porch steps. Not much taller than she was in her lowest heels, his compact body and springy movements reminded her of a leprechaun, albeit one with a Brooklyn accent.

She waved a greeting. "I brought dessert. And a few plants."

"Dessert? Now you're talkin'." Barney rubbed his hands together as his bushy white brows rippled with interest. "I'll take a peek."

"Oh, no you won't." Arms out like a crossing guard, Eden blocked his path. "Last time I let you 'peek' at dessert, you ate the peanut butter cups off the peanut butter pie."

"I did not." Seventy-four this past June, Barney pretended to scowl, but beneath wiry brows, his aqua eyes twinkled in childlike glee. "Not *all* of them. Besides, 'Eating is the best of prayers.' Avrunin said that."

"Who's Avrunin?"

He shrugged amiably. "Who knows? Someone on the Cooking Channel, maybe."

Eden laughed. Self-educated after high school, Barney was a walking treasure trove of quotes and interesting ideas. He and his wife, Charlene, had moved west from New York, settled in the Willamette Valley and eventually opened the Holliday Fish Market. For forty years, Barney had operated the retail end of the store while Charlene served the best fish-and-chips Eden had ever tasted. She used to stop by on her way home from work to relax a few moments with them, sitting at a small table in the back of the shop, nibbling on battered tilapia while they soaked their hands in the bowls of vanilla-scented water Charlene set out to take the smell of raw fish off the hands of all the fishmongers at the end of the day.

With no children of their own and no relatives nearby, the Gleasons considered everyone family. They'd been Eden's first friends in Holliday and had drawn her into their circle without hesitation, offering her a sense of belonging she had sorely lacked at the time. So, as the shops along Liberty Street set their sorry-we-missed-you signs in their windows for the evening, Eden enjoyed a few moments with Barney and Charlene, listening to them discuss pregnant Amanda Gibson's curious craving for mackerel, or how they could discreetly sneak more whitefish into Ron Wilcox's weekly order now that Ron was trying to make ends meet on social security. What she really waited for, though, every evening she dropped by, was the moment Barney dried his own hands, then reached for his wife's. Picking up a soft dishcloth, he carefully patted her fingers, the backs of her hands and her palms, then smoothed on a creamy lotion that smelled like rose water. At some point during the process, Charlene's head would tilt back, her eyes closing in contentment. When the hand massage was complete, Barney would drop a brief kiss on Charlene's upturned lips. Sitting up, blinking, she'd sigh, pick up the bowls of water, and together they'd finish closing the store for the night.

That was it. Very matter-of-fact. Completely mundane. And one of the loveliest moments Eden could imagine. Every time she watched the ritual, her heart squeezed with a yearning so deep it stole her breath.

"Flowers," Barney said now, surveying the profusion of blooms nestled in the cart she'd wheeled up the slab walkway. He poked a multi-petaled bloom. "These are the kind Charlie likes, aren't they?"

"Crimson mums," Eden confirmed. "I thought I'd come over Sunday to plant them."

"All right." Blinking quickly, he nodded. "She'll like that. You grab your bag, I'll carry the dessert." His smile deepened every line on his face yet somehow made him look younger. "Which I'm guessing by the gold box is from Sweet Holly's?"

"Correct." The year-old bakery in town had rapidly become Barney's favorite. Holly, the owner-head baker, had made dulce de leche *sufganiyot* for Hanukkah last year, winning Barney's eternal devotion.

"Devil's food?" he asked now, focused on the cake.

"With mocha buttercream and chocolate curls." Eden eyed him sternly. "I expect those curls to be on the cake when the other guests arrive."

"'Hope is the thing with feathers that perches in the soul'—Emily Dickinson," he quoted.

"'Sometimes the best answer is a simple yes or no.'—My mother," Eden quoted back to him.

Barney laughed. "Come inside. Charlie's waiting."

Eden followed him up the steps. The wooden screen door creaked in welcome as he opened it and stepped to the side, allowing her to pass into the brightly lit home.

The running joke among Eden's friends was that she'd flirted with every available male in Holliday between the ages of eighteen and ninety-four. When they said that in her presence, she would point out that she took in a whole lot more territory than just Holliday. The truth was that she rarely passed the flirtation stage with anyone. Shabbat open house at the Gleasons' was her regular Friday night date, and it was the best part of her week.

"I've got a chardonnay in the refrigerator. I'll open it and pour you a glass," Barney offered.

"Sounds good."

While he took the cake to the kitchen, she headed for the downstairs office they had recently converted to a bedroom when Charlene came home from rehab several weeks ago. Her steps slowed as she approached, and it took a conscious effort for Eden to tame the emotion stirring in her chest and bring a smile to her lips.

"Hi! Ready to play beauty salon?" she sang out as she entered the room.

In the center of a twin-sized bed, Charlene sat up against a stack of pillows that seemed to swallow her. At the sound of Eden's voice, her gaze shifted from the TV on the opposite wall, and she raised her left arm, fingers curling in a tiny hello.

Six months earlier, Charlene had suffered a

major stroke. Since then, Eden had made it a habit to arrive before the Gleasons' other guests, so she could spend a few moments regaling her friend with local gossip and futzing with her hair and jewelry.

Slipping off her heavy shoulder bag, Eden set it near Charlene's feet and lowered the protective railing attached to the side of the hospital bed. "I brought a new nail polish. It's called Passion Fire. Red with a hint of brick for the fall. You'll love it. Ooh, and wait'll I tell you what Livia Pullen suggested to the Thanksgiving planning committee today." She perched on the edge of the mattress. "Liv wants to put life-sized turkey statuettes on every street corner. Some of the committee loved the idea, but Janette Breem said they'll decorate this town with fake poultry over her dead body and that Liv was going to make us look like an episode of *Green Acres…*" While she talked, Eden removed items from her bag.

Every Friday, she packed makeup, hair pins and spray, an oval hand mirror and manicure supplies, including a few different shades of polish, and brought the kit and caboodle to Charlene.

"What should we do first today? Hair?"

Charlene's mouth worked laboriously. "You… choose," she said after considerable effort.

Scooting the medicine bottles on the end table over a bit, Eden set out nail polish remover and a baggie full of cotton balls. Prior to the stroke, Charlene had presided over Friday nights with boundless enthusiasm and the energy to match. Stirring pots, pulling braided challah breads from the oven, holding up bites of the rich stew she called *gavetch* and ordering, "Taste. On a scale of nine to ten, tell me how you'd rate it," she was the heart of their gatherings.

In the hospital and inpatient rehabilitation for four weeks and home for eight, her recuperation was, so far, slow and arduous. Friday night open houses had been suspended until last month, when Barney had decided his wife needed to feel involved as much as she needed to rest. Charlene didn't seem so sure about that. She didn't want people to see her this way, with the right half of her body paralyzed from her eyebrow to her toes. The lips that used to bloom in generous grins moved on one side only now, giving her mouth an odd, puzzled expression.

"Let's start with nails today," Eden decided. She knew a little something—more than a little, actually—about seeing shock and, worse, pity as people tried not to stare. It sucked. Long ago, she'd learned the value of redirecting their attention to where *she* wanted it. Maybe she couldn't change Charlene's reality, but she could help her friend thumb her nose at it a little.

"Jeremy is going to Europe for the entire month

of December. Did I tell you that?" Maintaining a newsy spiel about her boss, she polished nails, styled Charlene's dove-gray hair and slipped a favorite rope of beads around her neck. She finished with a judicious application of makeup, then held the oval mirror up for Charlene's inspection.

In Eden's eyes the courageous woman was lovelier than ever, her tenacity easily upstaging the remnants of her illness. But as Charlene studied her reflection, the flash of pain in her light eyes was impossible to miss. Eden's heart squeezed painfully in response.

Nodding, Charlene tried to smile. Half of her mouth obeyed. "Hot…stuff. Do again…next week."

"Absolutely." Eden pretended to believe the upbeat words just as Charlene pretended to mean them. "Next week."

"Ready for dinner?" Barney appeared at the door with a small meal set atop a breakfast tray, and Charlene's eyes lit with a much more genuine happiness at the sight of her husband.

As Eden started to repack her bag to make a space for the tray and for Barney, Charlene reached with her left hand to hold Eden's forearm. "*Thank* you"—which came out as *Tsank*—she worked hard to say. "You're a good girl."

Kissing Charlene's soft cheek, Eden moved to

the doorway so Barney could trade places with her at his wife's bedside.

From the threshold, she watched him set the tray on the bed, unfold a cloth napkin and tuck it carefully into the collar of the feather-soft zip-up robe she'd helped him pick out when Charlene was still in the hospital. Sitting so that he didn't disturb the tray, Barney bent his head close to his wife's and recited a hushed, private prayer for the two of them and God. Then he tucked a fork carefully into Charlene's right hand and said, "Eat, *bashert.* It's not too hot."

Eden knew he would stay until Charlene had as much as she wanted, or as little as she thought he'd let her get away with. Leaving them to it, she set off down the hallway to see if there were any tasks to complete before the Gleasons' other guests began to arrive.

Bashert. They'd been calling each other that as long as she'd known them. Once she had asked if the name stood for something, and Charlene had told her it was Hebrew for "meant to be." *Imagine,* Eden thought for the umpteenth time, *believing you found your meant-to-be and discovering that not even a lifetime could change your mind.*

In the kitchen, the cake she'd brought was sitting in its still-closed box next to the glass of wine Barney had poured for her. Opening the lid of the gold bakery box, she transferred the dessert to the counter and felt a pang of frustration. Certainly, the cake was pretty, its chocolate curls intact (thank you, Barney), but it wasn't homemade. It didn't say, *"Welcome, so glad you came, you're special to me!"*

Cooking had been Charlene's art, the canvas on which she'd painted their lives each week. When she'd first arrived in Holliday, Eden had bluffed her way through a bravado she hadn't really felt. Twenty-something, ballsy and gregarious, on-her-own-for-the-first-time-and-loving-every-second— that was the charade. The reality? She'd been a terrified, quivering mass of nerves, lonely as hell, confused and wondering if she would ever be truly happy.

Maybe Charlene and Barney had seen past her chirpy facade when they'd realized ordering fish-and-chips was becoming a pattern. Or perhaps being genuinely content had given them compassion to spare. Whatever the case, they'd pulled her into their world, inviting her to Friday night Shabbat in their home, where they lit candles, drank wine and discussed the complexities of life in a way that was utterly new to her. Eden's family was Jewish, but not observant, and family dinners were mostly a thing of the past for a host of reasons she avoided thinking about. But here in the Gleasons' home, there was friendship and laughter and food. Oh, the food! She'd made her first friends in Holliday at the Gleasons' Shabbat dinners, a stranger they treated as a friend.

Now the kitchen was silent, Charlene's ladles and slotted spoons hanging idly on their silver hooks, and Friday night Shabbats were potluck. Last week they'd scooped spinach dip out of a plastic container. Charlene, who had always made her food look as good as it tasted, would have had a conniption if she'd known.

Eden tapped her lip. Somewhere in one of the upper cabinets there was a lovely burgundy glass plate Charlene used to display desserts. Though Eden was the first to admit she'd never been able to cook worth a darn, she knew how to play dress-up and figured that if she put her purchased cake on a beautiful plate, maybe snipped a few of the crimson mums she'd brought and arranged them around the base, she could carry the dessert into the bedroom later to show it off and elicit genuine pleasure from her friend.

At five foot three, she didn't have enough leverage to reach the top cabinet unaided. Her T-strap pumps had piddly two-inch heels, and the Gibsons' cabinets extended all the way to the ceiling.

Tossing her coat on the peninsula, she pulled over a barstool, kicked off her shoes, hiked up the pencil-slim skirt that restricted her movements and climbed onto her knees atop the polished wood surface.

"Yikes." This might have been a bad idea. Heights were her kryptonite. In elementary school, she used to freeze at the top of the slide and refuse to move until someone called her mother to come get her. There were probably still graduates of Linwood Elementary who hated her for ruining recess. Even though this stool was no Mount Hood, and she was still on her knees, the nausea and shakiness began immediately.

"All right, on your feet," she commanded herself, refusing to give in to fear. How could she, when Charlene lay trapped inside her own body just two rooms away? Using the counter, then the cabinet doors for balance, she rose awkwardly, unsteadily to her feet. The stool wobbled.

"Oh, Lord!" Clutching the cabinet handle with both hands, she closed her eyes to make the room stop spinning.

"Hey there, need some help?"

Rich and masculine, the voice startled her despite its friendly tone, and her first impulse was to turn toward its source, but she couldn't move. Could. Not. Move. Couldn't even open her eyes.

"Hello-no-I'm-fine," she squawked, which was dumber than dirt, because a) she wasn't fine by a long shot, and b) plummeting to her premature death was bound to be more uncomfortable than the embarrassment of admitting she definitely *did* need help.

Silence loomed. Had the bearer of the friendly voice left the kitchen? Was she alone again? Eden opened her mouth to request—as loudly as she could—that he come back and help her to the floor in one unbroken piece when a large hand covered hers.

"Oh!" She didn't just move at that point, she nearly jumped off the stool. Her eyes popped open.

"Whoa," he soothed. "Nice and steady. I've got you."

The man beside her braced one broad, comforting hand against her lower back. With the other, he reached for her left hand, which had stupidly let go of the handle and was now flailing for something, anything so she could keep herself balanced. His smile was gentle and easy, an attempt to encourage rather than mock or belittle. From that point on, everything seemed to happen in slow motion. His fingers slid over hers like silk, applying only enough pressure to stop their trembling, and it all looked so graceful and beautiful and right that, ridiculously, this seemed like the perfect way to meet Brandon Buchanan in person for the very first time.

"Can I help you down?" he asked.

His voice. Like melted caramels.

"No." Hearing the raggedness in her own voice, she cleared her throat. "No need. I…only lost my balance for a sec." The fib emerged through quivering lips.

Most of the time, Eden viewed herself as a strong, some would even say kick-ass, woman. Promising herself she could pass out later if she needed to, she gave him a smile she hoped to heaven was dazzling.

His palm engulfed the back of her hand. As she looked into gentle hazel eyes, all she could think was *holy moly*. With gold-streaked brown hair— not too thick or long, just enough to be beautifully average—and palomino-colored skin that reflected the time he spent outdoors and was already forming laugh lines around his eyes and mouth, he looked perfectly imperfect. Just right for her. Hope flared in her chest.

"You sure you're okay?" he asked. Genuinely. Thoughtfully.

"Right as rain." She made her smile bigger.

"Do you need help with something?"

The timbre of his voice alone sent a thrilling vibration down the center of her body. He was so friendly! And his eyes... Hazel was such a kind color.

Feeling far too breathless and eager, she tried to ground herself in the mundane. "I need to get a cake plate down from there." Using her chin to point so she didn't have to let go of anything, including him, she indicated the top cabinet.

"Glad I'm here, then. I'm tall. Useful for reaching into high places." The easy curve of his lips spread into a full-fledged grin. Her stomach clenched, and this time it wasn't entirely from the fear of heights.

"How do you know Barney and Charlene?" she asked. And why hadn't she known they'd met him already?

"I've just been getting to know them, actually. I stopped in at the fish market one afternoon to ask if they'd sponsor a youth group I lead, and Barney and I struck up a conversation. I'm still pretty new to town."

"Oh, is that right? And… What kind of youth group do you lead?" she asked as if she hadn't read and reread the article a few dozen times.

Briefly, he described Community Kids. "How wonderful," she commended. And then in the cheesiest move of the millennium, she said, "On behalf of the city, I want to thank you for encouraging our local children." *Sheesh. Spread it on a cracker, Berman.* "I work at the Holliday History Museum. We're a nonprofit." Shameless, shameless, shameless, but she *did* work for the museum, and it *was* a nonprofit. "If you ever have fliers you'd like us to display or want to discuss something we can help you support, please don't hesitate to come in." *And ask me to marry you.*

"Great. Thanks. The name's Brandon Buchanan, by the way."

"Oh, sorry! I'm Eden Berman."

His left hand still held hers. As they tried to crisscross right arms to shake, the awkwardness struck them both as humorous.

Our first laugh.

For so long Eden had believed…no, hoped…no, *dreamed*…that when the right man came along, the slightly off-center feeling she carried deep inside would dissolve. The need to guard herself, to stay on her toes wouldn't be necessary anymore. Her soul would feel safe.

A river of warmth flowed from their clasped hands up her arm and into her chest. *Thank you, thank you.* Her future had finally arrived.

"Excuse the interruption. Barney said there was a wine opener on the counter."

And there went her bliss bubble. Turning to see Gideon Bowen gazing at them, gray eyes as chilly as winter, she blurted, "Where did *you* come from?"

Gideon raised one slow, dark brow. "Is that the only greeting they taught you in charm school?"

"No," she shot back without a moment's hesitation, "but they also said a lady shouldn't cast her pearls before swine."

Yeouch. The words were out, too late to retract them, when she heard them the way Brandon…

anyone…would. They sounded so *mean*. And she wasn't mean!

Gideon didn't seem fazed in the slightest. His mouth had hardly moved, but she could tell he was mocking her on the inside.

That was the thing about Gideon: he didn't have to say a word, nor did his stony expression need to change for her to know he'd been judging her from the moment they'd met. And it hurt.

She was going to confront him about that eventually, but this wasn't the time. She had a first impression to save.

"Gideon and I love to kid around," she told Brandon, forcing a laugh. "We have that brother-sister, tease-each-other-till-it-hurts thing going on." If he contradicted her, she'd bean him with a dinner plate.

"Oh, this is your brother." Nodding, Brandon grinned.

"No!" she corrected quickly. "Lord, no. My brother lives in Portland. He's wonderful." The words hung in the air until she became aware of the implication. "And so is Gideon," she lied, facial muscles tightening, "of course."

The look he gave her could have frozen fire. Looking away, she gave her full attention to Brandon. "My brother and I were best friends growing up. Still are."

"Imagine," Gideon muttered.

She shot him a side-eyed glance that said *Watch me ignore you*. Turning back to Brandon, she smiled with all the charm she could muster. "His name is Ryan," she told Brandon. "Ryan Berman. He's an architect in Portland. He works on ADA-accessible accommodations."

"No kidding? That's awesome. I have a brother named Ryan," Brandon shared with her.

"You do? What a coincidence."

"Yeah. I'm really close with my sibs, too."

"That's so nice. I love it when families are close." Logging the information in her More-to-Love-About-Brandon file, she asked, "How many siblings do you have?"

"Six. Four brothers, two sisters."

"Plus you? Big family." She had always wanted a large family, with the sound of laughter and squabbling emanating from every room in the house.

"Yep. I'm the third oldest. I have one older brother and an older sister." Courteously, he turned to Gideon. "How about you? Any siblings?"

"No." That was all he said despite Brandon's attempt to include him in the conversation, and if he could have looked more bored, Eden didn't know how.

"You're an only child?" she smiled at him. "Shocker."

"I used to wish I was an only child," Brandon

confessed amiably. "Growing up on an island with so many brothers and sisters, there was nowhere to escape."

"You grew up on an island?"

He nodded. "Off the coast of Washington state in the San Juan archipelago."

Eden smirked happily in Gideon's direction. *My future boyfriend is comfortable using the word* archipelago.

"I'm fascinated by islands," she told Brandon. "Each one seems to have its own *je ne sais quoi…* if that doesn't sound too pretentious."

"Oh, it does," Gideon muttered, and she spared him a glare, but Brandon was nodding, agreeing with her, so she continued.

"I would love to make a travel study of islands. Borneo, Mykonos, Grand Caymans—"

"Gilligan's."

She was going to slay Gideon with a butter knife. "Do you mind?"

"No, I don't mind. I came in to get a bottle opener. I have a Brunello di Montalcino that needs to breathe." He raised an expensive-looking wine bottle.

She rolled her eyes. And he thought *she* was pretentious.

"Why are you standing on a stool?" he asked, which—*crap, thanks a lot!*—made her remember that she was still several feet off the ground. Almost instantly her dizziness returned. *Damn, must remember to sign up for a hypnosis class.*

"Brandon is helping me get something down from the cabinet," she said. "Maybe we should—"

"Oh, yeah," Brandon agreed—*and let go of her hand.* "You wanted a cake plate, right?"

Oh, crud. Crud... Still clinging to the cabinet door with her right hand, her left now floating in space, Eden had the sudden, distinct feeling the stool was about to tip over. Instantaneously, there came a disturbing awareness of the distance between the ground and her skull.

Oh, dear...

This time, the nausea rose more quickly, filling her throat. *No, no, no, we do not want to vomit on our soul mate.* Briefly, she considered grabbing Brandon's shoulder, but she was afraid to move even that much with the room beginning to spin more quickly than her intestines. A soft whimper escaped her lips.

"Here we go...cake plate. Is this the one?"

Pardon, I need help she wanted to say, but the words would not come. Hell's bells. She was going to fall and crack her head open. When she looked down—which she definitely should not have done—the Gleasons' tiled floor appeared closer than it had been before. Closer...and inexplicably undulating. The edges of Eden's vision disappeared.

Oh Lord, she really was going to puke on her future fiancé.

"Breathe." The command sounded as if it came from far away. The voice was deep...hypnotic... or was that the dizziness taking over?

There was a loud crash...sounded more like glass than her body smacking the floor, but she couldn't be sure...then someone swore, and just as she wondered if she was about to experience great pain, she felt a pair of strong, solid arms circle her body and hold her tightly. Again, that deep voice spoke to her, comforting her. Surely it had to be Brandon—

"You're safe."

Oh, good.

In the sliver of time she had before passing out cold, Eden recalled it had been a very long while indeed since a man had held her. Her last conscious thought was, *What a shame I won't be awake to enjoy it.*

Chapter Three

"She's frowning. Do you think she's in pain?"

No, I'm not in pain.

Swimming up from unconsciousness felt like an out-of-body experience. Eden floated in a strange sea of thoughts ranging from *I wonder if I'm dead* to the conviction she was Hermione Granger and had just told Harry Potter, *No, you may not have my treacle tart, Harry. If you eat another one your teeth will fall out.* It was weird, kind of peaceful and rather entertaining. And whatever she was lying on… *Mmm,* soft as a cloud.

"Can she hear us?"

The speaker was male. He sounded both worried and kind.

"Open your eyes, Eden!" *Ew.* The second voice was more adamant, like an alarm clock. "Come on, it's time to wake up."

The unwelcome order and tone attached to it made her want to turn away, but when she tried, a pain in her neck elicited a wince.

Oh wow, a whole lotta pain was happening now. Her shoulders and upper back were sore, as if she'd lifted something heavy, and her neck flat out ached. What had happened? The last thing she recalled was feeling really good about something.

Trickles of memory teased her. A warm smile… a handsome face…the feeling of being in exactly the right place at exactly the right time…

She felt her eyelids flutter and had the strong urge to open them, but the closer she came to "awake," the less comfortable she felt.

The delicious softness she'd sensed at first turned out to be her own upper arm. She was lying on her side, her arm beneath her cheek. The rest of her body was supported not by a bed soft as a cloud, but by the hard, cold floor.

"What happened?"

"She's trying to say something."

Trying to?

"Barney, would you bring me any strong-smelling spice you've got? I'd like to wake her up."

I am up… wait… Barney…

That's where she was! She'd gone to the Gleasons' for dinner and had been having a really good time talking to—

"Brandon."

"What did she say?"

"I couldn't make it out. Say that again, Eden."

But she didn't want to speak again. Feeling an urgent need to wake up and find out what was going on, Eden blinked her eyes open and forced herself up. Or tried to. Her head quickly came in contact with something solid that blocked her path.

"Ow! Sonova—"

Barney grabbed her arm, steadying her so she wouldn't fall back to the floor. Kneeling at her other side, Gideon Bowen held a hand over his nose, eyeing her over the top. Apparently he'd been leaning very close to her face. "Are you all right?" he asked, his tone more wry than deeply caring.

"I'm fine." She rubbed her temple where it had connected with him. "I have a hard head."

"No kidding."

The trickle of awareness Eden had while waking up expanded as she took in her surroundings. She was at the Gleasons' all right, sitting up, with Barney's help, on the nonslip porcelain tile she'd helped Charlene pick out last year. How had she gotten here again?

"Can you tell me your name?" Gideon asked.

"Of course." She wasn't *that* far gone.

"Humor me. Your whole name."

"Eden Lea Berman."

"All right. And do you know who this is?" He nodded toward Barney, whose concern was scrawled across his face in long, deep lines.

In an attempt to alleviate the worry too often etched on her friend's face, she summoned a smile for him. "Barney Gleason."

"Good. And who am I?"

"Don't you know?"

He arched a brow, waiting.

Eden eyed the man who crouched beside her, one knee on the floor, the other bent, his elbow resting atop it. "Gideon Bowen, Lord of the Duplex."

He glanced at Barney. "She seems to be returning to normal. I'd like to listen to her heart and lungs. Would you mind bringing my medical bag?"

"Of course. I put it in the hall closet. Maybe you could take Eden to the sofa in the living room, where she can be more comfortable. I'll meet you there."

Rising on legs that had seen more limber days, Barney nodded at Eden. "It's good to see you awake. You gave us quite a scare, Edella." He used his affectionate nickname for her and smiled the sweet Barney smile that could comfort like a favorite blanket, but Eden could see the anxiety still in his eyes. Watching him walk out of the room, she realized she had zero recollection of him arriving in the kitchen. Last she remembered, Barney had been in the bedroom with Charlene.

Straining to remember details so she could piece together the events, Eden glanced around the kitchen. Brandon *had* been here, hadn't he? But if so, where was he now? She hadn't somehow dreamed it all?

"Did I pass out?" she asked tentatively, anxiety coiling in her belly.

Gideon's neutral expression returned. "What do you remember?"

The problem was, everything she could remember from the most recent past seemed distorted, as if it had happened in a dream or to someone else. There was Brandon, smiling…and he'd smelled like Irish Spring soap, which had made her feel happy and hopeful, but she'd felt anxious, too, because—

"I was standing on a stool, looking for something…a…a plate. Wait a minute—that's what happened. I brought a cake and was looking for something to put it on. Then Brandon came in, and we started chatting, but I got dizzy and felt like I was going to fall and… Brandon caught me!" She sagged with relief. "I *do* remember."

Stoic as ever, Gideon appeared not to share her triumph. "Do you remember what was happening right before you became dizzy?"

"Brandon and I were talking." She *had* to ask. "Where is he? And when did you get here?" she added, realizing she had no memory of Gideon's arrival.

Without responding to either of her questions, he slid his left arm beneath her knees, his right arm around her back, and stood.

Reflexively, Eden threw her arms around his neck. "What are you doing?"

"Taking you to the living room."

"I can walk," she protested, but Gideon behaved as if he hadn't heard her.

The exquisite awkwardness of being carried in the arms of a man she'd only ever battled with kept her silent as they left the kitchen, but her senses fired like pistons. Gideon was far more muscular than she'd previously guessed. Beneath a crew neck sweater, his chest, abs and arms felt...quite solid. He held her as if it was no effort at all.

As he carried her through the dining room, Eden became uncomfortably aware of the way her hands cupped the back of his neck. The short hair on his nape tickled her fingers, but she wasn't sure where she'd put her hands if she let go. Before she could decide, a flood of new images assailed her.

"You were there," she blurted, "in the kitchen with Brandon and me."

His eyes cut to her briefly. "Correct."

That was it? *Correct?*

In the uncomfortable silence that followed, Eden's senses heightened. She felt the way his body moved, and the scent of his skin seemed more prominent. Gideon used aftershave. It was faint now, but clean, not spicy.

"How long was I…unconscious?"

"A few minutes."

They reached the living room, where the fire crackled, casting a glow on forty years' worth of the Gleasons' photos and collectibles. Gideon lowered her carefully to the couch and was still leaning over her when he asked, "Are you comfortable?"

His good smell might have been partly pheromones, she thought, and then suddenly she knew. She knew almost certainly—

"It was you. When I fell off the stool, *you* caught me." Her breath seemed to stick in her throat. "Didn't you?"

Straightening, he gazed down at her. "I noticed you were gripping the cabinet tightly. And you were hyperventilating."

She nodded. "I'm afraid of heights."

The edges of his mouth turned into a barely-there curve. "The kitchen stool qualifies as a 'height'?"

"Yes." Heat crept into her face. "You obviously didn't get a good look at it. It's very high off the ground."

"How high off the ground?"

"Many feet."

His slight smile twitched at the corners. "That explains it, then."

Surprising her, he sat down on the edge of the deep sofa cushion. She quickly scooched over to make room.

"For future reference," Gideon said, "holding your breath or overbreathing from anxiety can both make you light-headed. We learned that in medical school."

"Puts those student loans in perspective," she murmured, earning a flash of humor that briefly warmed his metallic eyes.

Before they could say anything more, Barney bustled in, carrying Gideon's medical bag and a large pillow. "I told Charlene everything is fine, just a little Shabbat excitement. Good thing you were here, Doctor." He handed off the medical case, then tucked two pillows behind Eden's back.

"You don't need to go to all this trouble," she protested as he arranged the pillows to his satisfaction.

"Don't be silly," he scoffed. "We need to get you well."

"I am well." While Gideon concentrated on getting what he wanted out of his medical bag, Eden told Barney, "I'm so sorry I ruined the evening." And then, because it seemed as good a time as any to ask, "Where's Brandon?"

"More people were arriving, so I asked him to

tell them tonight was canceled and promised to call everyone later." His strong, knobby fingers squeezed her shoulder. "Don't you worry. We're focused on you here."

Eden could feel her mood begin to plummet. *Every party has a pooper.* So much for first impressions. Perhaps it could have ended worse, but she wasn't sure how. Self-disgust curled the edges of her heart. She'd spent half her teenage years learning way too much about medicine and hospitals and how easy it was for people to forget about you when you couldn't participate in the fun. As a result, she'd worked hard through the years to be the life of the party, not the death of it.

Placing the tips of his stethoscope in his ears, Gideon settled the bell on her chest, beneath the collar of her dress. "Breathe in, please," he told Eden.

"I'm fine now," she protested. Other than dishonesty, greed and discrimination, there were few things Eden hated more than being treated like a patient. "Not even dizzy anymore. You know what I think? I should go home—"

"If you could stop talking and take a couple of deep breaths," Gideon repeated, "I'd like to listen to your lungs."

"My lungs are perfect. I have no problem with my lungs."

"Eden," Barney chastised gently, "do what Dr.

Gideon says, for my sake. You gave us all quite a scare. A seizure is no laughing matter."

Say what? "A seizure?" she squeaked.

Barney nodded, and not even his reassuring presence could make the news less alarming. "It was—"

From the expression that crossed his face, Eden had the impression Barney was about to say something like "serious" or "terrifying," but Gideon intervened.

"We don't know yet if it was a true seizure," he corrected. "I suspect you experienced a vasovagal syncope accompanied by a brief convulsion, which can appear similar. Take a deep breath."

"Wait." Shooing the bell of the stethoscope away as if it were an unwelcome bug, she clutched the edges of her collar together. "Back up a second. I have no idea what you just said." As a rule, she didn't like talking to doctors—not when she was the patient! And, she'd been the patient far too many times in her life, beginning at the vulnerable age of fifteen. She'd learned then that too many doctors talked at you instead of to you, and she'd come to hate the feeling that she was just a body without a vested stake in the proceedings. "Vaso—what? Explain, please."

"Vay-so-vay-gul sing-co-pee," he pronounced carefully. "You may have felt anxious or fearful or…" He paused for a nanosecond. "…excessively excited, resulting in overactivity of the vagus nerve, which in turn can lead to a lowering of blood pressure and then to syncope. In lay terms, a fainting spell."

"A fainting spell. That's it?" She sagged with relief. "I had a fainting spell."

"With a brief convulsion, but that's not entirely uncommon after a syncopal event. Have you ever experienced a convulsion before?"

"What? No!" So much for her nanosecond of relief. "A 'brief' convulsion. How long would that have been exactly? Is that why my neck is sore?" Also, not to be shallow or anything, but what had it looked like, and had Brandon witnessed the whole thing?

She'd finally met the man of her daydreams up close and personal and had keeled over like a Tennessee fainting goat?

Her plan all along had been to wow Brandon first, then introduce him—slowly—to her shortcomings. Not bedazzle him with a full display of her weaknesses the moment they finally met.

Gideon's unemotional voice weighed in again. "Occasionally, someone will faint and experience a very short-lived convulsion. It can happen once and never occur again. The fact that it hasn't happened before is encouraging, but your physician will want to rule out heart or brain abnormalities as contributing or causal factors." He raised the stethoscope again, his dark eyes piercing. "May I listen to your heart now?"

Eden held the collar of her dress tightly, aware that she appeared more like a child refusing a pediatrician than an adult talking to a doctor. The mere thought of medical tests fired up a coil of nerves through the center of her body. Her life had finally been looking up, and if she hadn't climbed onto that ridiculous stool this could very well have been the best night she'd had in years. All she wanted to do now was go home and phone her brother and Nikki. They knew her better than anyone. They would understand why a medical issue—any medical issue—threw her into a mental tailspin. Her brother was good at calming her when fear took over. Maybe Nikki would come over to binge on *Gilmore Girls* and brownies.

"I think it's time for me to go home." She tried as hard as she could to smile at Barney, but felt her lips wobble.

Barney glanced to Gideon.

"I'm not comfortable letting you go without a cursory check of your vitals, at least," Gideon said, which elicited nodding from their host. "If you'd be more comfortable in the emergency room, I can take you."

"No!" More comfortable in an emergency room? Was he kidding? Barney looked as though he was about to second the emergency room motion, so she jumped quickly back to option number one. "You can check my vitals here."

Gideon waited while she very carefully unbuttoned only enough of her dress to allow the stethoscope access to her chest and upper back. She took deep breaths when he told her to, followed a light with her eyes and sat through the squeezing of his portable blood pressure cuff.

Finally, Gideon pulled the stethoscope from around his neck. "Everything checks out fine, but you'll want to follow up. Do you have a personal physician?"

A personal physician? Singular? Eden scoffed silently. For years her physicals had resembled a guided tour of Oregon Health & Sciences University.

"Yes, I do."

"If you give me a name, I'll call and—"

"That's not necessary. I'll phone first thing in the morning," she promised when Gideon frowned more than usual. "They always get me in quickly."

He mulled this over, eyes narrowing as if trying to gauge whether she could be trusted not to drag her feet.

Tugging the hem of her skirt so that it stayed mostly where she wanted it, Eden maneuvered her legs awkwardly around Gideon to perch on the edge of the couch. Whether they liked it or not, she was going home.

"Are you dizzy?" Gideon asked.

"Nope," she fibbed, but only a little. Her head felt kind of fuzzy, yes, but the room wasn't spinning.

"All right, then." He stood and said to Barney, "I'll take her home. We'll stop by the diner first for dinner."

"No," Eden disagreed baldly. *No way.* "No, *thank you*," she amended under Barney's watchful eye. "We can walk home together, sure, but I'm not hungry."

"When was the last time you ate?" Gideon questioned.

"Today." She saw him trade a look with Barney, who was almost as serious a food pusher as Charlene. Eden knew she needed to come up with a better response. When *had* she eaten last? "Lunch." Probably. It had been a busy day at work. "I have plenty of food at home."

"Low blood sugar can be a contributing factor in both syncope and seizures," Gideon said, winding the tubing around the headset of the stethoscope. "How about water? Are you properly hydrated?"

"Like a philodendron?" Both men looked at her blankly. She rubbed her cold hands together. "I drink a lot of tea."

At Gideon's request, Barney brought her a glass of grape juice, then insisted on making her something to eat, and the only way to avoid that was to agree to stop at Thanksgiving with Gideon on the way home.

"You make sure she eats a good meal, not bunny food," Barney told Gideon as they put on their coats for the walk to town. Then he wagged a finger at Eden. "And you follow doctor's orders."

Considering it prudent not to respond to that or to glance in Gideon's direction, Eden hugged her friend good-night and headed down the walkway with Gideon a silent presence at her side. They'd reached the sidewalk when he gently took hold of her elbow and directed her toward downtown.

Still without looking at her, Gideon murmured for her ears alone, "If I'd known it could be this easy to get you to cooperate, I'd have claimed 'doctor's orders' a long time ago."

Huddling in the single unisex bathroom of the homey seventy-seat restaurant on Liberty Street, Eden looked in the mirror as she waited for the number she'd tapped on her cell phone to ring.

She looked…meh. All right, under the circumstances. Her dark brown waves were mussed, too much of the natural curl coming through to have the sleek look she preferred. Beneath her brown eyes, her skin looked sallow, so she juggled the phone and her makeup bag to reapply blush and her signature red lipstick. Looking well, she had discovered, was more than half the battle when it came to convincing other people that you *were* well.

Gideon had insisted she have a bowl of clam chowder before they ordered entrées, so she was already fed. Hydrated, too. Physically, she felt perfectly normal again, no ill effects from her scare, but being with Gideon in this situation didn't make her feel emotionally normal at all; in fact, she felt uncomfortable as hell. He seemed to have talked himself out at Barney and Charlene's and was now content to order food she didn't want and watch her eat it.

"Excuse me! You've been in there an awfully long time. Are you all right?" Rapid knocking accompanied the high-pitched query.

"Yes," Eden responded to the voice on the other side of the door. "I'm fine. Thank you! Be out in a minute."

Refilling her makeup bag, she moved closer to the window, hoping her conversation would not be overheard. Disappointment deflated her when she reached Nikki's voice mail: "Hi, you've reached Nikki. I'm either healing the planet or out enjoying life. Leave me a message with all your details, and I'll get back to you." *Beep.*

"Niks," Eden said into her cell, "I'm at Thanksgiving with Gideon Bowen." That was sure to come as a surprise. As far as her best friend knew,

Gideon was still merely the Dark Landlord she tried to avoid. "There's too much to explain over the phone, but listen, I met Brandon in person tonight, and it was really nice at first. *Really nice*. But then it was pretty awful. I think. I mean, I was unconscious so I'm not exactly sure how he reacted, but it couldn't have been good."

Another series of raps on the bathroom door interrupted her. Eden covered the phone, called, "Be out in a minute!" and returned to Nikki. "Call me when you can, okay? Actually, call as *soon* as you can, because now that I'm alone with Gideon, I feel incredibly uncomfortable and need an excuse to head home. So call. With an excuse. Okay, bye."

Stealing another minute, she disconnected from Nikki and tapped her brother's number next. Four rings and his voice mail, too, picked up: "I'm having an exciting evening! Hope you are, too. If this is Eden, you'd better be doing something more interesting than watching *Shark Tank*. Call you when I can. *Ciao*."

Eden touched the red phone on her screen, not bothering with a message this time.

Another round of knocking, more urgent this time, preempted an additional call, not that there was anyone else with whom Eden felt comfortable sharing the fact that she'd passed out in front of Mr. Right and now felt…bizarre. The kind of bizarre she had felt for so much of her life, a feeling that she was not merely different, but inferior.

"Are you done in there, yet? I'm elderly, and I need to go!"

"Very sorry! Coming!"

Enough stalling. Gideon was waiting. Slipping her phone into the side pocket of her purse, Eden unlocked and opened the bathroom door.

The tiny, elderly woman on the other side glowered at her. "An eighty-five-year-old bladder is nothing to toy with, dear."

"No, of course not." Eden stepped out of the bathroom. "I'm so sorry." The woman pushed past her, shoving the door shut and clicking the lock. Eden headed down the short hallway to the dining room.

Thanksgiving was, as the name implied, decorated in autumnal shades of rust, gold and brown, warm and inviting. A river rock fireplace, double-sided, stood in the center of the restaurant with booths and four-top tables on either side of the large hearth. To counter the current chilly weather, flames crackled through real logs piled on the grate. She and Gideon had chosen one of the booths on the street side of the restaurant, close enough to the fire to see and feel the glow.

As she approached, she saw Gideon frowning in concentration at his phone. As always, his shoulders were squared, his back impeccably straight.

Firelight highlighted his dark hair, making it shine. Dressed in an ivory wool cable-knit sweater, he rocked the casual look, she had to admit. As she reached their booth and slid onto the bench opposite him, he glanced up.

"Good, you're back. I've been texting with a colleague, a neurologist, about follow-up for primary syncope with convulsion," he relayed without preamble. "If you give me your doctor's number, I'll contact him or her first thing Monday morning to convey my observations, your post-event vital signs, and make sure—"

Eden held up a hand. "Whoa. Pump the brakes, Speed Racer. First of all, I don't know my doctor's number by heart."

"It must be in your phone."

"No." She reached for her water glass, which she noted had been refilled. "We're not besties."

Gideon gave his head a brief shake. "It's simply the responsible thing to have your physician's number readily accessible."

Eden shrugged. "Responsible, overkill—that's such a fine line, isn't it?" She smiled to soften her words. "Look, nothing personal, but I don't run to doctors for every little thing. Hey, I thought of something," she said, hoping to steer the conversation off herself. "You were wearing a shirt and tie when you came into Holliday House this morning, but now you're wearing a sweater. Ergo, you went home to change clothes after work. Am I right?"

He set his phone to the side and eyed her quizzically. "What if you are?"

"If I am, then you should have arrived at Barney and Charlene's without your medical bag, because you'd have left it at home. You, however, had it with you. So you planned to visit Charlene at home *in a medical capacity.*"

Her revelation was interrupted by the arrival of their appetizers. She'd thought the chowder had been plenty, but hunger reasserted itself when their server set down a plate of golden fried macaroni-and-cheese balls plus a skillet of mini muffin-shaped meat loaves "frosted" with duchess potatoes. Her comfort-food faves.

"I'll let you work on those and check back in a bit," the young woman said.

Eden was tempted to dig right in, but the heat wafting off the macaroni-and-cheese balls persuaded her to let them cool while she returned to her topic. "So why did you make a house call tonight?"

"It's easier for the Gleasons that way."

She pointed her index finger at him. "But you don't like house calls. You think they're an overuse of medical resources and invite excessive insurance claims."

"How do you—ah. Janette Timmons."

"Nope." She shook her head at the mention of his medical receptionist. "Sandy Linstrom from the museum café. She's dating Miles Hart, your pharmaceutical rep." Eden shrugged at his look of profound surprise. "The Holliday grapevine. More reliable than NPR. Go on, ask me anything about you."

He scowled. "I'll pass." Nudging the appetizer plates toward her, he said, "Eat up, and we'll order dinner."

"Dinner?" She shook her head. "After all *this*? Not for me. This will be more than enough." She poked at a macaroni ball to see if it was cool enough for her to take a bite. "After the chowder and a plate of these babies, I won't even be hungry for breakfast tomorrow."

Gideon shook his head in disapproval. "It's not wise to run on empty all day. Your body needs fuel in the morning to keep your blood sugar level throughout the day."

"You sound like my mother."

"Your mother and I would get along."

Eden suppressed astonished laughter. He had no clue how right he was. Over the past twenty years, her mother had bonded with anyone in possession of a prescription pad. Eden did not, however, want to discuss her foible-filled family with Gideon; she was having far too good a time.

"Anyway, I *am* eating," she told Gideon blithely. "I said that I wouldn't be hungry. I didn't say I wouldn't eat." Picking up one of the golf-ball-sized treats, she swirled it expertly in its accompanying sweet chili sauce and took the first luscious, crunchy-gooey bite. Taking her time to savor, she waved the little nugget. "These better be served in heaven, or I'm not going. I love food. Especially breakfast."

"Your breakfast choices leave something to be desired. From a nutritional standpoint."

"How do you know?" She took another bite.

"Recycling. I've seen the boxes." He arched a dark brow. "Fruity Pebbles?"

The moment she swallowed, she argued, "It's vitamin fortified. And you shouldn't stalk other people's recycling."

He shrugged. "We share a bin. Someone has to break down the boxes. There's more room that way."

"There are only two of us. We don't generate enough recycling for the bin to fill up."

Gideon transferred one of the mini-meat loaves onto her plate. "There's a principle involved. When you break the boxes down, it's neater."

"Neater recycling. In the closed bin on the side of the house where no one but you and I see it."

Picking up her fork, she removed the meat loaf's puffy potato cap, ate it in one bite, then pointed the fork tines at him. "You need a hobby."

His smile appeared as if it was an afterthought. First, his expression remained neutral. Then his lips began to curve gradually and kept right on curving until his expression turned into a grin, and the grin turned into a laugh. It all seemed to happen in slow motion, but was worth the wait. Gideon laughed as if it was the first time anyone had ever done it, as if the very act surprised him.

"You may be right," he said, putting one arm across the top of the booth back, looking more relaxed than she'd ever seen him. "You certainly seem to enjoy *your* favorite hobby."

"Which would be?"

"Provoking me."

On the brink of denial, Eden felt her own laughter bubble up. "I have devoted a lot of time to that lately, haven't I?" It was a surprisingly nice sensation—the firelight, the food and this odd coziness with Gideon, of all people.

Aware that he'd been feeding her this entire time and neglecting his own meal, she dipped a mac-and-cheese ball in the chili sauce, set it on an appetizer plate and slid the dish toward him, licking sauce off her thumb.

"So," she said, crossing her arms and leaning

on the table, her smile easy and genuine as she enjoyed the gentle epiphany of connection, "should we be friends now?"

Chapter Four

Before Gideon could respond, a commotion a few booths away caught Eden's attention.

"Why do you have to be so pigheaded?" A petite woman with a halo of corkscrew curls surrounding her heated face blocked the progress of a man who was simply attempting to sit down to dinner.

Uh-oh. Eden knew that unrelenting blonde. And the beleaguered man who looked as if his primary goal was to avoid a stress-triggered stroke? That was Eden's own boss, Jeremy Holliday.

"Your great-great-great-grandfather and mine pictured our towns being one incorporated city."

Sophie Wurst, over a foot shorter than Jeremy, craned her neck to look up at him and spoke with her always expressive hands. "They envisioned a community where people helped each other. Where they cared about their neighbors—*all* their neighbors. Strength in *unity*, Jeremy. Not division." As always, Sophie sounded as if she was standing on the back of a train, delivering a stump speech. "It's time for our two great communities to come together. Solidarity." She jabbed her index finger into Jeremy's chest for emphasis. "*That's* the goal." Jab. "*That's* the North Star they wanted us to follow!"

Jeremy jerked a bit with each jab of Sophie's mighty pointer finger, but he kept his gaze leveled far above her head until she stopped speaking, whereupon he looked down slowly, focusing on her the way he might have zeroed in on a relentless fly he was itching to swat. "Our great-great-great-grandfathers loathed each other. Something I know you're aware of, *Sophronia*, because you have had your head buried in those asinine journals of yours since you were old enough to read."

Ruh-roh. Instantly, the macaroni in Eden's stomach turned into a cold, heavy lump.

"Our ancestors' journals are not asinine," Sophie pushed through clenched teeth. The crack and thud of a fallen fireplace log punctuated her statement.

"*Your* ancestors' journals," Jeremy countered blandly, as if unaware (which he certainly wasn't) that demeaning Sophie's heirloom family diaries would spark outrage. "*My* ancestors didn't record every sneeze so we could argue about who said, 'Bless you' a hundred and eighty years later."

Oh, damn.

Sophie's fingers curled into fists. Her chest rose and fell with audible breaths. "Take that back, Holliday."

Jeremy snorted. "Or what? We'll duel at dawn? I'm not going to take it back." Taking a seat in the nearest booth without another word or glance for Sophie, Jeremy raised his hand to catch the attention of Valentina, Felipa's daughter. "Menu, please?"

As aware as anyone in town of the enmity between Sophie (nee Sophronia) Wurst and Jeremy Holliday, Valentina sought Eden's gaze and made big eyes at her. *Do something.*

If Sophie and Jeremy continued to spar, it would not be the first time they drove the restaurant's other customers to resort to takeout.

Eden started to rise.

"You know them?" Gideon asked, his quiet, even demeanor a distinct contrast from Jeremy's at the moment.

"That's my boss," she whispered. "And that's Sophie Wurst. She lives in the next town over, and… Never mind, it's a long story. I'll be right back."

Masculine fingers curled around her wrist. "Your boss seems to be involved in a confrontation. As your…as *a* doctor… I suggest you stay calm tonight."

Eden glanced at her wrist, engulfed by his hand, the palm large and capable, fingers long and almost elegant. "A surgeon's fingers" her mother would say of that kind of hand. When she looked into his eyes, he released her immediately, which hadn't been her point, actually. It was the first time he'd touched her with anything other than professional neutrality, and she hadn't minded a bit. *Mental note: must get back to that question of whether we're going to be buddies now.*

She sent him a smile. "Don't worry. I'm calm. I'm always calm." His eyebrow said it all, and she laughed. "I'm not always calm with *you*." Leaning forward, she lowered her voice. "But I'm calm when it comes to Jeremy and his Sophie issues. This has been going on for*ever*, seriously. From when they were kids. Their families have been at war since the late 1800s, if you can believe that. It was practically a feud for decades, but it cooled down in the middle of the twentieth century. Rumor has it Sophie picked up the torch in grade school when she beaned Jeremy with a dodgeball in PE and called him a spoiled brat. He

retaliated by nailing her in the mouth with a Fris-
bee at recess. She cracked a tooth. They've been
at it ever since."

"They should be able to take care of themselves,
then."

She laughed. "You'd think so, wouldn't you, but
refereeing is part of my job description. No joke.
Jeremy asked about it in the original interview."

Before she could move or Gideon could protest,
Sophie slid into the booth opposite Jeremy, her expression as pugilistic as her fists.

Jeremy shook his head. "No. You are not sitting there." He gestured to Valentina. "She's not
sitting here."

Sophie smiled malevolently. "Want me to scoot
in next to you?"

"No! I want you to go home and find something
productive to do with your limitless free time."

"You know what your problem is, Jeremiah?
You're a privileged rich boy who inherited his family's sense of entitlement along with their ill-gotten
gains. The only reason I haven't sued you for the
hundreds of thousands of dollars your family owes
mine is because I am not litigious."

Eden tasted meat loaf in the back of her throat.
Once Sophie got on the your-family-stole-from-
my-family train, a wreck was inevitable.

"Steady," Gideon said, his voice low and firm,

as he correctly read her intention to intervene. "This is their business."

And yet Eden knew it was about to become the entire restaurant's business as Jeremy leaned across the table. "The only reason you haven't sued is because you know you'd be laughed out of court. Instead of trying to pad your bank account with other people's money, why don't you try novel writing? You seem to enjoy rewriting history."

Sophie's hand slammed the tabletop. "That does it." Rising from the booth, she called loudly, "Is there a lawyer in the house?"

Gideon reached for his wallet, dropped a fifty-dollar bill on the table and said, "Shall we?"

"Shall we what?" Noting Valentina's desperate gesture toward Jeremy's table, she whispered to Gideon, "Shall we kiss my job goodbye if Jeremy sees me walk past him without stopping to help?"

"If your boss has a problem with you not working during nonwork hours, I'll have a word with him. As a physician."

Well. She'd been used to advocating for herself. For a long time now. "Well, thank you, buuuut… no. Besides, that would mean *you'd* be working during nonwork hours," she pointed out.

They held each other's gaze, probably only for the length of a breath, before he smiled. Wow. He'd smiled more tonight than she'd ever seen. For a moment there seemed to be no one at all around them and nothing Eden had to do. Just a timeless, weightless moment of something like peace. Then Gideon slid smoothly out of the booth and stood, breaking the sweet spell. He really did intend for them to leave.

Eden sucked her bottom lip between her teeth, torn between what she wanted to do and what she thought she ought to do.

In ten years of working for the Hollidays, she had watched her boss practice stellar restraint as a way of life. In his everyday dealings, Jeremy was levelheaded, imperturbable and drama-free—almost to a fault. She enjoyed working for him, but trot Sophie onto the scene and—*boom!*—not only were the gloves off, Eden was unfairly expected to referee. She hadn't been kidding when she'd told Gideon she was good at remaining calm when he wasn't around. Her skill at mediation was practically legendary where Sophie and Jeremy were concerned.

Maybe it was the fact that Gideon's voice had eased tonight into something more human, more *humane*, than she'd been used to from him, or perhaps it was the sincerity in his steady gaze, or the fact that she'd been having a good time until Jeremy and Sophie arrived—something made Eden pause even as she was aware of Jeremy's mounting agitation. Since moving to Holliday, her job had become her identity, and if running interference for her boss was part of that, well, even Sophie had come to expect it.

Tension, like a piece of fabric pulling at the seams, filled her chest. For the past decade, she'd used work to fill the space her love life left blank. The trade-off had been conscious, deliberate, well tolerated. Until recently.

Sophie put a couple of sugar packets on the table and began to play sugar-packet hockey, using her thumb and forefinger to flick them as hard as she could at Jeremy. The first one hit him in the chest. Swiftly, Eden made a decision.

"Fine, let's go." Gathering her purse, she scooted to the edge of the booth before she could change her mind. To get out, they were going to have to walk right past Jeremy, who, if he saw his assistant, was certain to expect her to assist him in giving Sophie the boot. She'd pretend not to see them, that's what she'd do. "I hope you don't mind if rent is late next month," she told Gideon. "No telling how long it'll take me to find a new job."

Looking pleased, Gideon stood and reached into his back pocket. "Not at all, Ms. Berman." He took her elbow to escort her from the restaurant. "It's the little sacrifices that make a relationship like ours work so well."

This town spends more on twinkle lights than it does on public safety, Gideon mused as he walked beside Eden. He'd moved to Holliday because he'd been able to buy a one-doctor medical practice, where he could work mostly alone. His plan was to retire early, sell everything and spend the remainder of his days on an isolated few acres far away from the rest of the world.

He had not planned on Eden.

She walked peacefully beside him now, teasing, "Boy Scout," when he touched her elbow as they crossed one of the quiet streets. Despite the recent health scare, she seemed relaxed and upbeat, hands in her coat pockets, face tilted up to feel the night air, an unconscious smile on her beautiful lips. (That was an entirely objective observation.)

"You really like it here, don't you?" he asked unnecessarily. Eden was woven into the fabric of the town, as much a part of it as the corny year-round decorations.

"What's not to love?" she responded. "It's magical in Holliday, don't you think? Especially this time of year. The lights are so hopeful. It looks like thousands of stars fell from the sky and landed on the trees."

"All right."

She laughed. "Cynic."

He didn't mind the moniker. The shoe fit. Or it usually did.

Tonight had been a revelation. He'd told himself he was going to keep his distance—from everyone—do his job, go home, repeat. Once Barney and Charlene had become his patients, however, the line between personal and professional had begun to blur. Gideon had relied on personal contacts and pulled some favors to get Charlene the treatment he'd have wanted for a member of his own family. In turn, Barney and Charlene supplied him with free seafood and had insisted he join them tonight for Shabbat. It had meant too much to them for him to decline.

When he'd entered the kitchen to find his tenant standing on a stool, blushing as the big guy held her hand, Gideon had felt…anger. He'd been to just enough therapy to know that anger was only the surface emotion, that another feeling had to lie beneath. He'd ordered himself to be ruthlessly honest and had been forced to admit to himself that he was jealous. Or envious. Nothing wrong with being honest. If he'd met Eden fifteen years ago, he might have fought for someone with her fire, her unrelenting individuality. Her killer body. Today, he was honest enough to know nothing would ever come of the attraction. Nothing, ever. He knew he had to stay away. But then she'd fainted and convulsed.

That business in the restaurant about becoming friends… No. It wasn't going to happen. Still, he was a doctor and couldn't turn his back on someone with a medical condition. So, here they were.

As they walked along Liberty Street, he felt her

studying him, not even bothering to be discreet. Once, when he'd made an obligatory appearance at the chamber of commerce meeting to introduce himself as Doctor Shlessinger's successor, his reluctant presentation had received, at most, a lukewarm response. Afterward, Eden had chatted amiably with him and a couple of CC members, but when they were alone, she'd put a hand on her chest and said, "Personally, I enjoy a Count Dracula vibe. It may be a little severe for Holliday, though, a titch too 'I'll be drinking your blood for dinner later.' In the interest of patient retention, you might want to warm it up a bit."

He hadn't laughed at the time, but it seemed funny now.

"You're staring at me," he accused dryly as they walked, though his gaze remained on the street ahead.

"Why yes, He Who Has Eyes on the Side of His Head," Eden admitted, "I am. I consider myself a student of human nature."

"Do you."

"Yep. Sometimes I stare into your window at night. I'm on a mission to find out what you do at home that's more appealing than getting to know your neighbors."

"See anything interesting?"

"Not really. But the *Duck Dynasty* jammies look good on you."

The woman made it hard not to smile. He did his best. They walked a few more steps with her pretending not to watch him and his pretending not to notice that she was watching him.

"You're grinning on the inside," she needled as they passed beneath an old-fashioned cast-iron streetlamp. "Admit it. You think I am so fun, and you wish you'd started off on better footing with me, because then I'd invite you over for karaoke night and let you sing lead on Chicago's greatest hits. But no, sorry, you have not yet earned that level of devotion, my friend. You can have the Justin Bieber toe tappers. I'm hoarding the classics."

After a long, comfortable moment of silence, he replied, "'Saturday in the Park' is Chicago's best song."

Eden nodded. "I agree. If you want to sing that one, you'll have to bribe me."

"With what?"

"A bag of Thunder Canyon sea-salt and olive-oil kettle chips. The twelve ouncer, not one of those itty-bitty Barbie doll bags."

Gideon winced. She really needed to overhaul that diet. "I get heartburn just standing next to you. Why do you hate your arteries?"

"I don't hate them. I said 'olive oil.' That's healthful."

He shook his head. "A great figure doesn't mean you're immune to coronary artery disease. And it's quite possible the syncope was a result of low blood sugar, since your eating was admittedly erratic today."

"Stop, I'm blushing. You had me at 'great figure.'"

He stiffened instantly, sure he should have said something else. But he'd noticed. She wore clothes that often covered her from neck to shin yet hugged every curve like a lover.

"Don't worry, bub." Looping her arm through his, Eden smiled up at him. "I know you don't have designs on me. You'll be delighted to know I'm not the least bit attracted to you, either. We're perfectly safe with each other." She gave his bicep a friendly squeeze. "Isn't that nice? Relaxing?"

"Immensely," he muttered. It ought to be.

"So, Gideon, tell me, is it possible for anxiety to make someone have that syncope thingy?"

"Yes, anxiety could contribute to a syncope thingy," he responded, glancing at her as they passed beneath another streetlamp. "Why? Are you under a great deal of stress?"

"Mmm. Not really. I've been working overtime a little. You know how it is."

"Yes." Actually, her nerves had seemed sky-high when he'd entered the Gleasons' kitchen tonight, but he wouldn't let himself get personal. "So that was your employer at the restaurant."

She nodded. "Jeremy Holliday. His family

founded the town in the 1850s. They still own a lot of real estate and several local businesses."

"And the young woman he was with… Sophie?"

"Her full name is Sophronia Wurst, but everyone calls her Sophie. Except Jeremy. He likes to refer to her as 'Beelzebub's BFF.'"

"Harsh."

"Yeah. They tend to feed off each other. The history of the Hollidays and the Wursts is pretty fascinating," she said. "Or it is to me. I took US history as a minor in college. In fact, the history of the Northwest in general is really intriguing. Portland has a checkered past, you know."

"I've taken the Old Town Ghost Tour."

"Have you? That was very lighthearted of you."

"Is that a compliment?"

"Absolutely. What did you think of the tour?"

"Very enlightening. It reminded me that cities can be as complex as the people in them. First impressions are frequently incorrect. You can't take anything at face value."

"Okey dokey, not lighthearted, then." She laughed at him. "If you want a serious look at the city's past, I highly recommend the Portland Underground Tour. Lawlessness, scandal and troubling examples of ethnic crimes that make you realize why Portlanders are so committed to change."

In the light from the streetlamps, her eyes

danced merrily, and he heard himself the way she must have heard him. He hadn't always been so bloody serious. "I'll have to look into it."

"If you want company, I go to Portland all the time," she offered easily. "My family lives there. And my brother's getting married soon, so I'm in the city a lot on the weekends now. I'm the best woman." She grinned. "I look adorbs in my tux. Anyway, I could get tour tickets. I have a friend from college who's one of the guides. No pressure, just…you know, I like tours."

She'd make the offer to anyone who was going solo, he guessed. Two more pieces of information about Eden: always up for adventure and thought people who were alone might be lonely. He wasn't going to allow himself to wonder whether she was correct. "You were telling me about the Hollidays and the Wursts," he said.

She gave him a knowing look yet allowed the change in subject. "Yeah, the Hollidays and the Wursts. Back in the day, the rift literally divided the original town into two sections—the north and the south. The north remained Holliday. The southern portion was renamed Wurst, after Sophie's great-great-great-grandfather Samuel."

"Why did Sophie say the Hollidays owe her family money?"

"Because she believes they do. Wurst has never been a fiscally successful venture. Honestly, the town's been dying for decades despite generations of Wursts trying to keep it going." Eden huddled deeper into her wool coat as their shoes clicked along the cobblestones. "Back in the mid-1800s, Josiah Holliday and Samuel Wurst were best buddies who moved west together with their young families. Josiah had a little money and Samuel had knowledge of the timber industry from the time he spent working in a mill in Michigan. They started the first steam-powered mill in the Pacific Northwest, supplying lumber to gold mines in California. Samuel had the know-how, but Josiah had great business acumen."

"Sounds like a successful partnership."

"It was, for a time. They wound up owning all the land that's still Holliday and Wurst, though at the time they called it Concord—as in getting along harmoniously. Which turned out to be pretty difficult, because they had vastly different personalities and approaches to life. Josiah was clever, even shrewd. Samuel was more of a people person."

"What was the breaking point between them?"

"A romance. Samuel's son Abraham fell in love with Josiah's only daughter, Celeste. They were still teens and absolutely desperate to marry—very Romeo and Juliet—but neither family was fully on board. The kids decided to run away and— this part is according to Sophie's family diaries—

Abraham took a small fortune in family jewels and gave them to Celeste, instructing her to hide them until they could make their escape. Then they planned to sell the gems to bankroll their new life together."

"And did they?"

"No. Samuel had begun to run low on his own funds and asked Josiah if he could borrow against the company to help Abraham build a house for his bride-to-be, so they could keep the kids local. Josiah said absolutely not, reasoning that he'd been warning Samuel for years about his lack of thriftiness. But Samuel didn't equate helping others with irresponsibility. He was very philanthropic and gave away a large portion of his earnings. He and Josiah fought, and Josiah admitted he had no intention of allowing his daughter to marry Samuel's son, who wanted, by the way, to become a teacher—not a particularly lucrative profession. That's when the two men ended their friendship and came up with the idea of splitting Concord into two towns—Holliday to the north and Wurst to the south. Samuel walked away from the lumber mill and got into brick molding, but he was never successful. Business wasn't really his passion. He envisioned Wurst as a haven for people who were looking for community and a new start. Josiah, on the other hand, placed ads in newspapers on the East Coast, inviting 'industrious and forward-thinking people' to move to Holliday and start businesses."

"I've been to Wurst." Gideon nodded slowly. He ran a sort of pop-up clinic there for a significant number of uninsured families; it was his favorite part of the practice. "There's quite a large immigrant population."

"Which is exactly what Samuel envisioned. Sophie shares his vision, I think. A fair number of the residents are undocumented, and they tend to lie pretty low. When they can, people move out because Wurst is so economically depressed. There are far better opportunities elsewhere. Unfortunately, Sophie's been no more able than her ancestors to turn it around."

"And what happened to the couple?"

"Celeste's parents got wind of her plan to run away with Abraham and sent her to Europe with an aunt and uncle. A little over a year later, Abraham got a letter telling him Celeste had married someone in England. He never truly recovered. Some records suggest the loss triggered or maybe exacerbated a mental illness that plagued Abraham the rest of his life. He's the author of the diaries Sophie is so fond of."

"And the gems?"

"So again this is according to what Abraham shared in the diaries. Celeste wrote to him one last time after she married to tell him the jewels were still in Holliday House. But the letter was never produced. All anyone has to corroborate that assertion are Abraham's journal entries. To his credit, Josiah allowed Abraham and Samuel to search his home. Nothing was ever found. Abraham believed Celeste chose a hiding place her snoopy parents wouldn't find."

"Why didn't he ask her?"

"I think he might have, but she died in childbirth in England."

Gideon blew out a breath. "And to this day some people think the jewels are still hidden?"

"No, only Sophie thinks that. The Hollidays always maintained the entire notion of missing jewels was the product of melodrama and Abraham's mental unfitness. And honestly, the story disappeared from local historical accounts for years until Sophie pored over the diaries and brought the old business up again." Sighing heavily, Eden stated with dramatic wisdom, "It all began with a star-crossed couple. Romance can be treacherous."

"Word," he agreed dryly.

Surprised and obviously pleased by his response, Eden bumped shoulders with him. "Want to share your romance war story?"

"Nope."

She laughed. "You will eventually, you know. We're neighbors." She squeezed his arm. "And good friends. Friends share everything."

Gideon refused to rise to the bait and instead stuck to the subject at hand. "If Sophie's the one with the diaries, how do you know so much about them?"

"She showed them to me."

"Why?"

"Hoping I'd go to bat for her, I guess."

"Go to bat for what purpose?"

"She wants to get inside Holliday House so she can search for the jewels. She thinks they're hidden inside the walls."

That came as a genuine surprise. "So let me guess, Sophie would like you to convince your boss to let her look for them?"

"No, silly. She'd have to take the place apart brick by brick. She knows Jeremy would never agree to that. She wants me to sneak her in."

Alarm bells went off. "Are you considering that?"

"No. I like my job, remember?" They reached a narrow passageway between two buildings. "This is a shortcut back to our place, did you know that?" she asked him, aware that her hand was still curled around his bicep.

"No, I didn't know."

"Yep. This little alleyway cuts through three blocks. Then you turn right on Julian Avenue, left on Loretta, walk one block to Jackson, and we're home."

Gideon hoped his expression conveyed his doubt. "That's a shortcut?"

She nodded, grinning. "Trust me."

They entered the corridor, which broadened in some areas and narrowed in others. Gideon was proving to be mighty fine company—attentive, wry, curious. Eden was having a good time.

"This is…unusual," Gideon commented, his inflection suggesting "weird."

"It's supposed to be private and romantic."

He glanced down at her sharply. Without letting go of his arm, Eden laughed. "I didn't mean for us. I meant in general. It's Holliday's version of Lovers' Lane."

Gesturing toward the walls, Eden spoke over her shoulder. "No one knows the original purpose of this corridor. Honestly, there doesn't seem to be any legit reason for it. None of the storefronts open onto it. It's in one of the older portions of the town, so no one with an answer is around anymore. People used to dump wrappers and bottles and junk in here. About eight years ago, the Holliday Aesthetic League made it their annual project. They added the sconces, all the planters, and even wrought iron love seats. Then they renamed it 'Lovers' Lane.'"

"That sounds like inviting trouble."

Turning, Eden walked backward, facing Gideon.

The amber glow cast by cleverly placed sconces illuminated his features, his serious expression so… Gideon…that it made her laugh. "I think that's why they bought *iron* love seats. Super uncomfortable. There's a Valentine's Day tradition now. You eat dinner at The Arbor—very ritzy, you should try it." (She knew he hadn't, because the owner of Holliday's most upscale eatery was in her book group.) "And after dinner, you stroll through Lovers' Lane, which will have been decorated on your behalf with flowers and, if you planned well enough in advance, framed photos depicting the highlights of your relationship."

Gideon's grimace stated quite clearly, *That's the cheesiest thing I've ever heard.* She ignored him. "Then you reach a love seat where a bottle of champagne and the best chocolates in town are waiting. You can guess what happens next."

"You get drunk in an alley?"

"No! You get *engaged.* And you take a selfie." She clasped her hands beneath her chin to croon, "And it's shown on the local news at eleven, and all your friends and family call you and squeal. And you live happily ever after."

He didn't grimace this time; he looked pitying. *Well, harumph, Gideon.* Full disclosure: the tradition in Lovers' Lane was exactly how she imagined Brandon proposing. And why not? They lived here, worked here, would God-willing raise wee baby Buchanans here.

"You really do enjoy history, don't you?" he asked.

"Well, duh. I curate the museum and historical library." She rolled her eyes. "Sheesh, dude, pay attention."

"Stop walking backward. It's not safe," he said, twirling a finger in the air, directing her to face front, which she did, grinning.

"You're going to drive your children insane, you know," she called over her shoulder. Dropping her register, she mimicked, "'Walking backward isn't safe, kids. Turn around so Daddy doesn't have to scrape you off the concrete.'" Switching tracks abruptly as a thought occurred to her, she turned to face him again. "Ooh, I almost forgot to tell you one of the best traditions of Lovers' Lane, or maybe it's a superstition, and actually I don't know if there's any statistical evidence to back this up, but if you get kissed here unexpectedly—and it has to be unexpectedly—the tradition is you'll get engaged within the year. Isn't that sweet? I mean, really, you have to admit we have some of the most—"

Her word waterfall was stopped abruptly by— and, yeah, this was unexpected all right—*Gideon's lips*. On hers. Like...kissing on hers.

Okay, maybe not "kissing"? Maybe more like...

pressure…for a second. Very nice pressure. His lips were the perfect balance of soft and firm. Something zinged inside her, as though the kiss plucked a piano wire deep inside her chest, and it reverberated all the way down to the pit of her stomach. Her brain scrambled. *Okay, whoa. Get hold of yourself.* In what universe would Gideon Bowen, Ice Prince, kiss an effusive, emotionally messy woman who clearly drove him crazy? What was happening here?

"You said it had to be unexpectedly," he answered her unspoken question. "Good luck." Then he started walking again. That was it.

She stood still for a couple of more seconds, then stalked after him. "Wait a minute. Are you saying you kissed me so I could get engaged?"

"You seem to like the concept of love. Should you find your…*soul mate*—" said with his usual irony "—I'll be able to re-rent your side of the duplex, preferably to a very quiet, cat-less tenant with better eating habits."

Okay. *O-kay.* This was not the way she'd pictured their friendship forming, but she could flex. She certainly hadn't anticipated a zing of attraction to Gideon. Or maybe it was reaction. Whatever. Nothing to worry over. This spiced things up… made their relationship very *moderne, n'est-ce pas?* She began to smile, falling into step with him.

"You don't want to get rid of me, Gideon. You

would miss complaining about my recycling habits. I'm the cinnamon on your snickerdoodle."

"You're what?"

"The spice, my friend. Without cinnamon, a snickerdoodle is just a sugar cookie. Decent enough, but why settle for decent when you can fill your cookie jar with exciting?" He rolled his eyes, and she smiled more widely. "Do you want kids, Gideon? I could see you with a couple of rug rats. Of course, you're going to have to overcome your fear of, you know, *sound*." No response. "I've always wanted kids, which will probably alarm you given my admitted ambivalence over parenting the cat, but he's like parenting Draco Malfoy. He doesn't have a name—have I told you that? He just kinda showed up, and I kept expecting to find his real mommy or daddy, so I've never called him anything but Cat. If he sticks around much longer, I'm going to dub him Malfoy. That fits, don't you think? Who's your favorite *Harry Potter* character, Gideon?"

More silence. She stopped walking and turned, but Gideon had paused several steps back. Hands in his pockets, he gazed down at the cobblestones, his dark brows pinched together. Something she'd said?

"You okay?" she asked. He looked up slowly. "I can be a little verbose," she admitted.

The left corner of his mouth rose ever so slightly,

a crooked smile that softened the hard lines of tension on his face. "No kidding."

"Should I not have mentioned kids?"

The tiny smile slid off his face. He looked unbearably weary. "I don't want children."

As abrupt and final as the revelation was—quite obviously intended as a period in this conversation, not a comma—it cracked open the door to friendship a little bit more. At least it did from her perspective. She filed the information away, aware that the wisest course of action was to leave it for now. "Okay. I'm sorry. I didn't mean to—"

"It's fine, Eden." He shrugged. "Let's get you home."

Deciding against continuing the shortcut through Lovers' Lane, Eden guided them back to the main blocks that led home. After walking companionably for a time, she ventured, "I could direct you to some very good resources if you'd like to know more about the Hollidays and the Wursts. If you dig far enough, it's almost as dramatic as the Hatfields and McCoys."

Gideon nodded slowly. "Sounds like worthy nighttime reading."

"Yeah." That's what her nights consisted of when she wasn't at the Gleasons or out with Nikki, or at some community meeting—a whole lotta reading.

The urge to see Brandon again hit like a gale-force wind. Then again, her apartment would die of shock if a man other than a relative walked in.

Friendship with her next-door neighbor would be nice, but friendship wasn't enough. If she planned to hold her own babies someday, to curl up beside a man who was the love of her life and marvel at how easy it was to be happy, she needed to get down to business.

It was time for change—true change, not merely her usual modifications in makeup or hair color or clothing, the superficial alterations that gave her a sense of moving forward without really changing anything. Unless she missed her guess, the man walking quietly beside her could stand to make a few changes in his life, too, but that wasn't her business. She had to focus on herself. No more waiting. No more fear.

Okay, a whole lotta fear, but she was going to put herself on the romantic firing line anyway, because big rewards required big risks. She was ready to crack open her heart again if that meant letting love in.

Chapter Five

"No, I'm not wearing that! Are you nuts? Why do you even have it? Shoo. Skedaddle. We'll talk tomorrow."

About fifteen minutes after saying good-night the first time, Eden faced Gideon on her front porch. Standing in her open doorway, she stared, utterly aghast, at the credit-card-sized device he held in his hand.

"This is a medical tracker," he explained again, less patiently than he had originally. "It has a fall detector. All you have to do is wear it like a necklace—"

"I *told* you, I sleep in the buff. No clothes, no jewelry, no medical alert devices."

"This is about safety."

"This is about overkill. I'm not wearing a baby monitor."

"It's intended for seniors."

"Not a selling point, Gideon."

"Be reasonable."

Eden felt her eyes narrow unhappily. "Yes, absolutely. *Reasonable* is my middle name. It's getting late. I'm going to go to bed, so I can get a full night's sleep. I think that's a reasonable response to a fainting spell. Wearing that thing—" she shook her head darkly at the device in his hand "—not so much."

At first, seeing him on her threshold twice in one night had been intriguing, particularly as up to now he'd knocked on her door only once the entire time he'd lived here. The realization that he was here only to push his medical gadget on her, however, had dampened her hospitality. Play the role of hapless patient to his Dr. House? She crossed her arms over her chest. Nothin' doin'.

Gideon's chest rose and fell in controlled frustration. Holding the alert device, a stethoscope and a blood pressure cuff, he stated. "I'm coming in."

"Nah, not tonight." Eden smiled, sorry she'd already kicked off her heels as she tried to make her five-foot-three frame fill the doorway. She could be every bit as obstinate as he.

Okay, that was childish. Gideon was, after

all, trying to be a responsible doctor, but he was doing it by attempting to turn her into a responsible *patient*, and that was unacceptable. For much of her life, she'd felt like a patient. Enough was enough. She was damn good and ready to feel like a woman.

"Tell you what," she said, studying her landlord, "I'll open all the window shades as soon as I get up tomorrow. That way you'll know I'm alive and kicking. It'll be like our secret signal." No change in expression. "That's what's called a compromise, Gideon. Now you say, 'Good idea, I can live with that.'" The Mount Rushmore impression persisted. Time to pivot. Leaning her head against the doorjamb, Eden said in a tone as sweet and silky as chocolate cream pie, "You know, Gideon, you've been…well, pretty incredible tonight. I'm definitely going to stop bad-mouthing you to the locals."

His gaze turned assessing. "Have you been doing that?"

"*Nooo.* A little. But only in regard to your landlording style." His brow arched dubiously. "I *may* have mentioned a personal preference for warm-and-fuzzy doctors at the last junior chamber of commerce meeting," she admitted. "But that was almost a month ago, and I am now fully prepared to talk you up at our fall brunch. You're welcome."

She straightened away from the doorframe. "Alright, nighty night."

He took a step closer to the threshold, and this time she could see the barest hint of...something—Was it worry? Concern?—flit across his expression. Something fluttered in her chest... But it didn't matter. She did *not need a caretaker*. "I'll stay until you can find someone else to be with you overnight."

Dropping all pretense of patience, Eden contended, "I don't need someone to be here overnight. I've lived independently for a long time, bub."

He raised the medical emergency device and wagged it in the air like a pendulum.

"What are you saying—that's my choice? Get a babysitter or star in a Life Alert ad?"

"You're very dramatic."

"Save the sweet talk. Look, you and I share a common bedroom wall. If anything happens, I'll knock *very* loudly and wake you from a sound sleep." She raised three fingers. "Girl Scout's honor."

"You lost consciousness tonight, Eden. You terrified Barney and frankly, as a dedicated Scout—and the only doctor around for miles—you should know I can't leave you alone without precautions." He gave her a meaningful look. "And imagine the damage it could do to my medical reputation."

The irony turned his eyes a deeper gray. It wasn't lost on Eden that the man who wanted to remain as isolated as possible was also refusing to leave until he ascertained that she was safe. Add "integrity" to the list of Gideon's finer qualities.

"All this and a kiss, too," she murmured. "You know, I get that the kiss was just a friend thing—"

"It was a desperate I've-got-to-unload-this-tenant-before-she-makes-one-of-my-blood-vessels-burst thing."

"Whatever. The point is it was a very blah kiss any way you slice it. You may be out of practice and should brush up a bit. I'm not suggesting myself, mind you. I'm sort of spoken for. But I have girlfriends who could help."

"Nice try." He held up the device. "I won't be deterred."

"Give me the damn thing," she acquiesced badly, plucking the medical alert device from his hand. "Since my chance of winning this argument is a negative number."

Graciously resisting the opportunity to gloat over his win, he said, "If you're comfortable with my coming inside, I'll show you how this works." Pulling his cell phone from his back pocket, he began scrolling. "The pendant connects to an app on my phone. It uses a process called trilateration to determine physical location, plus has Wi-Fi and fall detection."

"What a nerd." Stepping back, she let him pass. His face was tight with concentration as he studied his phone and continued to explain trilateration—which interested her not the slightest—in careful detail. A reluctant smile tugged her lips. She closed the door. "How do you feel about Flake bars?"

"Hmm?" he murmured, distracted. "What's a Flake bar?"

"I did not hear that." She followed him into the living room. "A Flake bar is culturally relevant chocolate, Gideon. It's one of the things you eat while watching *The Crown*, *Downton Abbey*, *The Accident*—okay, granted it's a little hard to eat while you're watching *The Accident*, but most other British dramas pair nicely with Flake bars and sausage rolls. Oh, and I know where to get a wonderful Treacle tart if you're into the *Harry Potter* series."

He raised his head, brow furrowed. "You have a menu for watching TV?"

"You don't?" She wagged her head. "I can see we have a lot of work ahead of us, Gideon. A *lot* of work."

He was not "getting involved."

Gideon stood in Eden's kitchen, fixing the pilot light in her stove, which she'd mentioned (just tonight) had gone out. When he'd asked how long it had been out, she couldn't even remember. He'd told her how dangerous that could be, then went back to his place to get a microfiber cloth and a long-wand lighter, neither of which she had. Eden was in the shower; the pilot light could be fixed before she got out. He was being a responsible landlord; that was all.

About that kiss, his conscience prodded.

Using the cloth to wipe off some grease under the stovetop (guessing Eden had never looked under here, either), Gideon reminded his tyrannical conscience that the kiss meant nothing—to either of them. A kind of joke. That's all. He'd decided before moving to Holliday that his role here would be to administer good-quality medical care to the locals while making health care to the underinsured residents of Wurst a priority as well. That's it—nothing personal involved.

After cleaning one burner, he turned his attention to the others.

Before moving to Holliday, Gideon had gone whitewater kayaking alone on the Deschutes River near Maupin, where the class IV rapids were guaranteed to give him a workout, maybe drown him if he was careless enough. At that point, he hadn't much cared, but he'd quickly found himself fighting the water, battling with nature, arguing with God, except he'd been the only one yelling.

"I used to believe in You," he'd shouted above the cacophony of waves slamming into his kayak.

"I thought You wanted me to heal people. Well, I tried. I tried, and I'm done!"

Even as the raging water had tossed his kayak like a wild mustang attempting to throw a rider, Gideon had continued to rail against whatever Higher Power was out there. "How about your part of the bargain, huh? What happened to healing? Where's your peace and comfort now?" He'd gone to church with his family as a kid, never questioned a thing. Life had been easy back then, so why not believe in benevolence? But life could turn on a dime and when it did, faith began to feel foolish.

He'd decided on no more emotional investment. No more personal involvement. None. That was the new agreement he'd made with life. Take it or leave it.

That had been over a year ago, and Gideon had not veered from his course. He was a good medical practitioner—careful, methodical, studious. But the handholding was over, and the results of his efforts were none of his damn business. "Never let the patient get between you and the door." He'd thought that was heinous advice when he'd first heard it; now he lived by it.

Finishing the cleaning, he lit the pilot, tried all the burners, made sure the fan and lights were working on the hood and left the kitchen. Eden had made it clear she wasn't going to call anyone to stay with her, and that was her concern, not his. Maybe she'd use the monitor; maybe she wouldn't. Again, her choice. Bringing it over had probably crossed a boundary.

He'd heard the shower turn off a while ago and figured she was hiding out, waiting for him to leave. He flipped off the light in the kitchen, but figured he'd leave a small one on in the living room in the interest of safety, so she wouldn't trip if she woke up and wanted a glass of water or something more to eat in the middle of the night. He was a landlord; he was supposed to make sure people didn't trip on his property.

As he walked, the wood floor squeaked in places, seeming loud in the quiet apartment. There was no sound of TV, no talking, and when he reached the edge of the short hallway, Gideon saw that Eden was indeed in her bedroom. On her bed. Curled on her side, facing the door, wearing pink pajamas with avocados on the bottoms, she was snoring…not all that softly.

Gideon halted at the door. Eden had showered off her makeup; it was the first time he'd seen her without her typical glamorous look. In the past several months, he'd discovered there was a great deal more to his tenant than met the eye. She was funny, sassy, irreverent, uncontrollable. Beautiful.

And absolutely off-limits.

Her possessed cat had clearly staked out his side

of the bed and blinked malevolently at Gideon. "Don't worry, I'm not staying," Gideon told the feline quietly as he entered the room and reached for the quilt folded neatly on the foot of the bed. The bad-tempered animal hissed loudly and jumped to the floor.

Pulling the quilt over Eden, Gideon paused briefly, remembering the feeling of being at dinner with her and listening to her stories as they walked down that ridiculous alley. She wanted to be friends. He wished he could, with every fiber of his being. But it just wasn't possible.

"Sorry, Eden," he whispered.

Turning, he walked softly back to the living room and sat on her sofa, where he intended to stay for a couple of hours, just until he was satisfied Eden was having a good night. This did not qualify as "getting involved."

For just a moment, he closed his eyes. When the image behind his lids became a woman's enthusiastic smile as she informed him that all television shows got their own menu, he did the unthinkable— allowed his shoulders to relax, felt himself smile in return, imagined sitting on her couch and letting her chatty play-by-play of whatever they were watching (and she would deliver commentary, he was sure of it) fill his chest with pleasure.

It was a harmless few seconds of imagining. By morning, he'd be back in his own apartment, living his own life, minding his own business. Letting his secrets poison everything good.

Shortly after 1:00 a.m., Eden awoke with a start when the cat decided to bond by pretending her feet were mice and attacking them through the covers. "Cut it out, demon spawn," she grumbled, moving her legs and immediately realizing her mistake when he pounced harder. "For crying out loud." Shoving off the quilt, Eden rose to forcibly escort her roommate to the door, which she intended to shut in his furry little face until she noticed that a living room light was on. Trudging down the hall to turn it off, she nearly had a frigging heart attack at the sight of a man's shadowy form on her couch. Not only that but there was snoring going on.

Gideon. He must have stayed because she'd refused to call someone to come stay with her. The man was a control freak. A very sweet control freak.

"Gideon. Hey," she whispered, thinking she might poke his shoulder to wake him, but she just as quickly rejected that idea. Trying to send him home would only result in an argument, and they were both too tired for that. "We'll go with option number two," she said softly to Malfoy (after tonight's attack on her appendages, that was definitely going to be his name) as she accompanied her back to the hallway. Carefully opening her creaky linen closet, she withdrew a pillow and blanket, then returned to tuck the pillow as close as she dared to his head and cover him with the blankie. Instead of leaving immediately, she watched him while he snored.

Gideon was so…inconsistent. Abrupt and cold one day, thoughtful and concerned about other people the next—as if he couldn't decide who he wanted to be. But that was okay; she liked people who were idiosyncratic. Anyway, it felt nice…comforting…to know that the landlord next door cared about her well-being a little bit. She'd been right about Gideon being an odd duck, like her.

Maybe after she helped him thaw out a little more, she'd set him up with one of her girlfriends. Someone stable and mature, but not too stodgy.

"Come on, Malf." Scooping up the cat, Eden headed back to bed and crawled beneath the covers, but her mind was too full to allow her to fall back to sleep. While he destroyed her quilt by kneading it with his claws, she reached for the tablet she kept on her nightstand (pretty much summed up what she did in bed) and turned it on to google "How to attract a man." As articles popped up, she settled back against the pillows. "Listen to these titles, Malfoy. 'How to Tell If He's Ready for Marriage.' 'Why Men Lose Interest After Sex'— yikes—and 'Is It Meant to Be? Five Signs Mr.

Right Is Ready for a Relationship—With *You*!'"
She sat up straighter. "Okay, grab a pencil," she
told the cat. "I'll dictate, you take notes. This is
good stuff."

At some point, she had fallen asleep, tablet
pushed to the side and her cheek smooshed into
the pillow, mouth open so that when she woke to
a bedroom filled with gray morning light, there
was a circle of drool on the pillowcase.

"What time is it?" Raising only her head, she
craned her neck to look at the clock. Ten a.m.
"No!" She was supposed to meet Nikki in an hour
and had to shower, do her hair and makeup, get
dressed and caffeinate herself. The cat, who was
no respecter of weekends, always woke up her up
by dawn or shortly thereafter. "Great time to flake
out, Malf," she complained, then realized he wasn't
in the bedroom anymore.

Grabbing a hair tie from the nightstand, she
twisted her tangled locks into a messy bun and
headed toward coffee, wishing she'd practiced better sleep hygiene last night. She was tired. It had
been worth it, though; the loss of sleep was a fair
trade-off for the exciting info she'd gleaned from
"Five Signs Mr. Right Is Ready for a Relationship—
With *You*!"

She'd even pulled out her journal and titled a
page "MARRYING BRANDON BUCHANAN"
bullet-pointing items in the article. Rather pre-

meditated, yes, but matters of the heart sometimes required a small push. Nikki, a school counselor, worked with him at the high school and regularly fed Eden info. Now that Eden had an article to work from, they could look for specific clues about how ready Brandon was to fall in love. Anticipation put a spring in her step.

Once in the hallway, she remembered what was different about this morning: Gideon had slept on her couch last night, which was sort of weird and sort of cool. Would he, king of the early risers, still be here at ten? Hurrying to the living room, she was able to answer her question with a definite *no*. On the sofa, the blanket she'd put over him sat neatly folded, the pillow on top and Malfoy lying on the pillow as if it was a throne.

There was no sign that Gideon had been there at all, save for a note he'd taped to the door. Stripping it off, she read, *"Good morning. Your cat has been fed."*

Her head whipped toward Malfoy. "He fed you?" The cat, which Gideon had appeared to detest, opened his eyes and gave a very relaxed, nearly soundless meow. *Hmm.* Eden kept reading.

"I trust you're feeling more like yourself. Please continue to eat and hydrate adequately. As discussed, you should contact your PCP at the earliest opportunity and request an appointment."

Holy constipated personality, Batman. Despite

what Eden considered to be great progress in their relationship, he'd reverted to uptight *Downton Abbey* overnight.

"In the interim, I strongly suggest you limit or avoid intense exercise, solo outings to isolated areas and all driving until cleared by your physician. Do not hesitate to get in touch with questions, or if I may be of any service.

"Kindly, Gideon Bowen, MD"

Kindly, Gideon Bowen? Do not hesitate to get in touch? "We share a duplex, dude. If I need something, I'll bang on the wall."

Tempted to suggest to Gideon that he also should see a doctor—for immediate removal of the stick up his ass—Eden decided to practice restraint. It was probably wise to remember that Gideon didn't seem to have any friends and therefore might not know how to sustain the vibe. As far as she could tell, he hadn't entertained a single guest since he'd moved in, which she saw as both incredibly sad and a tantalizing challenge.

Adding *socialize Gideon* to her mental to-do list, she started a pot of coffee and headed to the bathroom to get ready.

A moment after she turned on the shower, a blur of white streaked past her. Malfoy. He loved running water. Go figure.

Eden stared him down. "We've talked about this. I shower alone." Holding open the bathroom door, she jerked her head toward the hall. "Out you go."

Her roommate stretched out a leg and began to lick himself leisurely. The poster child for cat adoption month. She nudged him with her foot. He bit her slipper. Hard.

Eden was an inexperienced pet parent, but she knew enough not to pick up the cat when he was moody (which was roughly 90 percent of the time). She'd often thought she'd get a dog someday, a big friendly one that her kids would be able to cuddle with for comfort and dress up in tutus. Life had happened, though—lots of twists and turns. No dogs, no kids, no tutu.

Giving up on expunging Malfoy, she adjusted the water temperature to lukewarm—not her favorite shower experience, but one her body could tolerate.

Stripping off her clothes, she started to step beneath the spray, then halted. Generally she hopped right into the shower without so much as a glance toward the mirror. It was easier to begin the day that way.

On a sudden, strong impulse this morning, however, she turned off the spray. Her heart pounded hard enough against the wall of her chest to make the moment feel dangerous, risky as she walked the few, interminable steps to the mirror.

The cat looked up, glaring. Eden glared back. "No photos."

Of course, she looked in mirrors every day. To perfect her hair and makeup, she studied herself at every angle, but from the neck up. *Only* the neck up.

I fully and completely love and accept myself.

She'd learned the affirmation during a spate of therapy sessions in her twenties and had used it on and off though the years. It didn't have a prayer of working as well when she was buck naked as it did when she was wearing, say, a fabulous M.M.LaFleur sheath dress. She'd spent years buying clothes to distract herself and everyone else from what was going on underneath the clothes.

I fully and completely love and accept myself, and I forgive myself for not looking like Gigi Hadid in a string bikini.

Breathing in and exhaling deeply, Eden reached the wide, framed mirror above the vanity. At the last second, however, she turned coward and closed her eyes.

Be brave. Love yourself. Know your worth.

Others had said the words to her. She'd said them to herself, half convinced she meant them, but her self-acceptance had always been conditional, as if secretly she'd been waiting for the day she'd twirl amid a flutter of sparkles and fairy dust and become the Disney Princess version of lovely.

Never gonna happen.

Living with the reality of a damaged body for the past twenty-one years should have made acceptance easier. It didn't. Probably because she'd become so very good at practicing avoidance.

Take a breath. Open your eyes. Let it be okay.

Ready? On the count of three. One...two... three...

Maybe four...

On ten she opened her eyes.

Her inhalation was so sharp, it hurt. As always, the shock of seeing her skin, once so smooth and taut, felt shocking. Commanding herself not to glance away, she tackled the much harder task of trying not to judge. Her life was divided into two parts: Before The Car Accident and After The Car Accident.

Like smocking on fabric, the skin across her stomach appeared to have been stitched—poorly. Unnaturally pink and unevenly puckered, it covered her belly, left side of her rib cage, left hip and upper thigh. An article of clothing she'd donned at age fifteen and could never remove, it had been defining her for too damn long. And judge it she did. How could she not when every magazine, every love scene in every movie, every flipping Victoria's Secret Angel, even an innocuous backyard pool party, had the power to make her dizzily, nauseatingly self-conscious? She'd gone to therapy, rubbed vitamin E oil on the scars to "make friends with them," and a long time ago had taken a chance on the faith that she could be loved for exactly who she was, exactly how she was.

That spectacular dive into optimism had led to a marriage. And a divorce.

Eden figured she could count on the fingers of one hand (with a couple of digits missing) the times she'd stood naked in front of this mirror in the ten years she'd lived in this apartment. The flood of feelings that rose threatened to sweep her away every time.

Watching her own chest rise and fall shallowly, she attempted a belly breath—in for four counts, out for five—willing herself to calm down, to be as objective as humanly possible.

Keloid and contracture scars covered approximately 40 percent of her torso. That left 60 percent smooth skin across her shoulders and half her back, plus a decolletage that was nothing to sneeze at. Her breasts were softly rounded, 34C, still plenty perky, so no complaining allowed. Backing away from the mirror in order to expand her view, she assessed her legs. The scars on her left thigh weren't pretty, but they didn't extend very far, and the rest of the skin on her legs was smooth and ivory-colored, because tanning was strictly out. She did Pilates four times a week whether she wanted to or not, partly to maintain her figure and partly because the lengthening stretches countered her body's tendency to tighten around the scar tissue. Overall evaluation of the gams: good. Quite good.

An extendable mirror was attached to the wall. Pulling it out, she turned around and angled it so she could assess things from the back. Shooting the side-eye to the cat, who continued to watch her disdainfully, she said, "Yeah, like you're not self-involved. Don't judge."

Okie. Dokie. Booty view. Be objective.

Pretty damn nice, actually. The scars on her back were less pronounced. And the shape of her tushie? Fine. Mighty fine. (Thank you, squats.) Also, her dark hair was thick and wavy. If she could somehow back naked into Brandon, she might stand a chance.

Her sigh was loud and long. Shoving the mirror back into place, she headed to the shower, once again adjusting the water to a dissatisfying tepid, because her scar tissue, which ran deeper than the surface as scar tissue tended to do, was giving her pain lately. She already had a doctor's appointment to discuss this issue and would mention the "convulsive syncope," as Gideon termed it, on the same visit, even though she loathed the idea of having one more thing "wrong" with her.

Stepping beneath the spray and pulling the shower curtain closed, she let her mind wander.

When Charlene was in the hospital after her stroke, Barney had stayed by her side constantly. Forty years of companionship had been visible in every move the man had made—in the fingers that had wrapped tightly around the rails of the hospital bed; in the way he'd stroked the back of her limp hand, as if he was afraid to hurt her yet desperately needed the contact; in his interactions with doctors and nurses; in the too-rapid blink of his exhausted eyes as they'd strained to note the slightest improvement.

The first time Charlene had smiled, only one small section of her lips had managed the conscious movement, turning her formerly generous grin into a befuddled-looking grimace. Tears had filled Barney's eyes. "My *shayna maidela*," he'd said to her, his voice hoarse and adoring. "My beautiful girl." He'd meant it.

Maybe it took decades of companionship to see the beauty in every wrinkle and jowl or distortion life brought. Maybe it took the act of loving with your soul.

Standing in the shower's mist, Eden imagined loving and being loved "forever," history and mystery woven into a fabric that became more beautiful with time. It sounded rare. Elusive. But if it was possible at all, then how could she not search for it?

The water couldn't wash away her scars, but as

it sluiced over her, she imagined a March rain, carrying away the long winter of her fears and ushering in a much-awaited spring.

Chapter Six

Nikki Choi had been Eden's best friend since the day they'd both stood in line to squirt mustard on their pizza in middle school. They'd bonded over that shared quirk and had been bonding over food, careers, relationships and their insecurities ever since. Today they were meeting up with her brother and his fiancé, Olli, who wanted to show Nikki a wedding storyboard, whatever that was.

After showering and opting for more casual hair and makeup than she usually did given the time crunch, Eden poured two very tall thermoses of coffee, added a generous amount of hazelnut creamer to each and toasted two bagels, slathering them with cream cheese and packing them to go. Everything was ready by the time Nikki arrived.

"God bless you, God bless you, God bless you." Nikki reached for the bagel as Eden got in the car.

"Does Drew know you take a break from the keto diet when you're with me?" she asked, buckling up so they could hit the road.

"Oh, we're not only keto anymore," Nikki said around a mouthful of chewy bagel. "We're full carnivore now. Drew says it's the single best approach to leaning up quickly. He encourages all his clients to go carnivore. I'm at nineteen percent body fat."

"Wow." Nikki was indeed much more fit than she'd been in all the time the women had known each other. Nik had always had the rounded curves of her Mayan birth family, plus a hankering for the tartes tatin, challah and bibimbap with which she'd grown up. Born in Guatemala, she'd been adopted by her Jewish Franco-American mother and Korean father. Their home was a lush blend of each other's adopted cultures and faiths—food included. That richness had seemed like an intrinsic part of Nikki. Or, she *used* to have rounded curves and a love of simple carbs. A personal trainer by trade, her fiancé was helping her "clean up and lean up"—which was his business slogan: "Clean Up and Lean Up with NorthrUp!" The phrase was blazoned across the side of his Chevy Suburban and printed on every shirt Eden had ever seen the man wear.

Eden had her doubts about their relationship, but maybe that was envy talking. Her scars weren't going anywhere, after all. Couldn't keto those babies away. Her body was already the result of multiple surgeries and years of healing. This was her. And hooray for the body-positivity movement and everything, but would she alter her appearance if she could? In a New York minute.

"Where's Drew today?"

"He's running a 10K in Bend, then giving a talk on organ meats as a higher fuel."

Good Lord. "You've always been gorgeous," Eden said honestly. "If I had a body like yours *before* you got down to nineteen percent body fat, I'd never complain again as long as I lived." She took a deep swig of sweet coffee and admitted, "Although that's probably baloney, because my inner Jillian Michaels keeps telling me I can improve."

Nikki glanced over. For a while there was only the sound of her Ford Escape's tires spinning across the pavement. Then she said, "Thanks for that. Also, Josh was a putz."

Nearly spewing her second sip of coffee, Eden laughingly agreed. "Yeah, he was." Joshua Grant, her high school sweetheart and, later, husband, had hooked up with Eden's Yoga For Fertility instructor in the sixth year of their marriage. Eden had always wanted to have children and had thought Josh wanted that, too. Because scar tissue tended to grow over time, creating barriers to fertility, Eden had decided to do all she could to address her concerns about conception and pregnancy. At that point it had been nine years since the car accident, three since her last surgery to minimize scarring. Her pelvis had been fractured in the crash, and she'd still had pain. Yogi Jenni had been interested and so helpful.

Turned out that when your husband left you for someone who practiced paddleboard yoga in a string bikini, you developed a different kind of scar tissue. A kind that wrapped around your heart.

"So, you had a bite to eat with the landlord?" Nikki asked curiously.

Glad to focus her mind on a much happier topic, Eden launched into a play-by-play of the previous evening's fainting spell, Gideon's assurance that it was a syncope thing, and their dinner at Thanksgiving. She stopped short of the walk home.

"And now we like him?" Nikki's emphasis on "like" implied *like*.

Fact: Gideon's kiss was the first one Eden had had in years. Nikki would be all over that info like fleas on a dog. Eden was not going to go there. The kiss was platonic and…cute. It was a cute thing to do. Making a big deal out of it would be a mistake and a distraction from the real focus of her life.

In that spirit she responded, "Yep. Very nice guy as it turns out. And a conscientious doctor. Pretty handy to have one next door. Guess what I discovered about Brandon?"

"What?"

Eden described the "Five Signs Mr. Right Is Ready for a Relationship" article.

"I can say yes to three of the five signs," she told her friend, ticking them off on her fingers. "He smiles often, he talks to you about his family and he touches you."

"He touched you?"

"Yes. Well, we shook hands."

"Hmm."

"For a long time. He lingered."

Nikki stared straight ahead, her tension transferring to her driving. They sped past a Mustang and a Tesla Model S.

"Whatever you're thinking, you'd better spit it out before you blow your wedding budget on a speeding ticket," Eden muttered.

Immediately, Nikki pulled her foot off the gas. "I'm so sorry!"

Eden shook her head. "Not a problem." Fortunately for her, post-traumatic stress had always centered on doctors and medical procedures, not the car accident that had put her in the hospital and kept her there for over a month. She'd been asleep in the back of her family's SUV when the accident had occurred, knocking her unconscious. Her brother, Ryan, had been awake and aware they were careening off the side of the road. He'd been soaked with sweat the first time he'd been in a car after the accident. Eden, however, had no memory of the incident prior to waking up flat on her back, lacking any sense of time or place or the slightest understanding of why she was in a hospital—groggy, weirdly numb in some places yet in others feeling the most excruciating pain she'd ever experienced.

Oddly, in all these years, car travel never bothered her. That was a silver lining, she supposed.

Chewing the inside of her lower lip, Nikki appeared to think carefully before she spoke. "I don't know, Edie. I don't know how much to say. God knows I'm not the poster child for body confidence, but… We never talk about it anymore, but I think the negative beliefs you have around your scars still make you believe you have to settle for, well, less than you would ask for otherwise."

Eden was genuinely dumbfounded. "Throwing my hat in the ring for Brandon Buchanan qualifies as 'settling'? In what galaxy?"

"That's not what I—" Nikki shook her head, her frustration palpable. "I'm not saying this right at all. I don't think any human being is worth less than someone else. And Brandon is a great guy. It's just that…" Still, she hesitated. "Can you be sure you're bringing your best, most whole self to a relationship when part of the appeal—a big part— is your belief that he's attracted to underdogs?"

Oof.

"I like underdogs, too," she contested. "It's not a character flaw. The world needs more people who are tolerant and accepting."

"Yes. The world also needs more people who believe they deserve a helluva lot more than to be tolerated and accepted. You don't have to be Giselle Bündchen to be loved."

"Says the woman who just lost thirty pounds at her fiancé's urging." The gloves were off.

"Thirty-seven, as a matter of fact. And Drew didn't 'urge' me." Nikki's perfect black brows plunged like crows diving for corn. "I wanted to lose weight—and I didn't do it so he would love me. He already loved me. I did this for me, because I want to feel— " She stopped herself, cutting the thought off at the knees.

"What?" Eden challenged. "What were you going to say?" Receiving no response, she felt sure she knew what Nikki intended. "You want to feel beautiful on the outside. You want to feel like the girls we envied in our twenties, right? The ones who could walk down a beach in a bikini, smile at a man and be sure he was smiling back because he liked what he saw. You want to believe that, finally, nothing needs fixing, and I get that. I *so* get it. I'm grateful you can experience that, but I can't. I'm never going to look normal, not remotely." Before Nikki could respond, she pointed a warning finger. "And don't tell me not to use that word. I don't look *normal*, Nikki, and I don't feel normal. That's not self-hatred—it's honesty. I'm protecting myself by being realistic. I need a guy with a big, big heart. That's one reason I like Brandon so much. So he's kind to people who aren't exactly average? Good, because I need that. And I'm not going to apologize to you for it!"

Silence slammed down on the car, like a lid over a still-boiling pot. Several minutes and as many miles passed before Eden glanced over. Nikki's jawline used to be soft, her cheeks round and luminous when she smiled. After weight loss, her face had acquired an angular elegance, the jawline sharply defined. Eden could see easily see tension tightening every muscle. She could also see when Nikki's tension began to melt.

"Tell me more about the article," her friend said quietly. "How to tell if the guy you like is attracted to you."

It was a concession. In over a decade and a half of friendship, they'd never had a heated argument. The car felt heavy with unspoken misgivings, yet there didn't seem to be a good reason to continue bickering.

"It's a questionnaire," Eden murmured, trying

to resummon her enthusiasm. "Since I've never seen him interact with other women, I thought…" She shook her head. "You know what, never mind. This is juvenile."

"No. Tell me," Nikki implored. "I'm sorry I analyzed you. You're right, you're my friend. My best friend, not one of the kids I counsel. I want you to have what you want, Edie. Tell me about the questionnaire. Since I've seen him interact with other women…" she prompted.

The idea of having Nikki answer the questions had sounded fun, exciting even, this morning, but now Eden just felt silly. "It occurred to me that if he interacted with me last night the same way he acts with everyone, then my results don't mean much, so I thought that if you answered the questions, too, based on what you've observed at school, it would be more accurate, but now that sounds absolutely ridiculous. You know what? I'm going to pull up my Victoria's Secret big-girl panties and ask Brandon out. Damn the torpedoes, right? A little rejection never killed anyone."

"He's nice to everyone," Nikki responded instantly. "Not flirtatious, though. Michelle Alessi— she teaches French I and II—was complaining about that in the staff room the other day. Brandon wasn't there, of course. Michelle said, 'Zat man, eee does not flirt. Why ees zat?'

"And Clay Rudolph—I told you about him, he

teaches physics and AP chem—is smokin' hot and would *love* to date our Mr. Buchanan. Clay's been commiserating with Michelle that he hasn't gotten a flicker of interest out of Brandon, either."

Conflicting threads of thought wove through Eden's brain. On the one hand, this all seemed like very good news; the questionnaire suggested that Brandon was giving off availability signals to her and not to the others. On the other hand, maybe he didn't want a relationship at all. Tempted beyond her control, Eden referred to her notes. "Do you see him leaning into anyone when he speaks?"

"Hmm, haven't noticed. Hit me with something else."

She glanced at her notes. "Have you heard him telling anyone about his family?"

"No."

A flare of hope kindled. "Does he touch women—appropriately, of course—when he's speaking to them?"

Nikki's brow furrowed as she thought. "Can't say I've ever seen him do that. But you said he held your hand."

"For longer than necessary."

"Well, there you go. That's good."

"Right. Of course, I was about to fall off a stool," Eden allowed in the interest of full disclosure.

"Did he check his cell phone while you were talking?"

"No. Ew, I hate that."

"Exactly. So that's still good."

"Okay, one more," Eden said. "To your knowledge, does he generally try to make women—or one woman in particular—laugh?"

"Well, in the staff room he's usually discussing Appomattox or why student test results are statistically unreliable. I would have to answer no." Her brows rose. "You're smiling. I take it he *did* try to make you laugh?"

Eden nodded. "He was very engaging. Really fun and…adorable."

With one hand on the steering wheel, Nikki reached over to squeeze Eden's hand. "Then I'm happy for you. I am. And I'm not just blowing sunshine, because I was skeptical before. I think you should go for it."

Eden knew she'd have pursued Brandon with or without her friend's encouragement, but with felt so much better than without. "You think you and Drew will be at the Holliday Hanukkah Party?"

"Absolutely."

"Good. I was wondering… How many dates do you think a person should have with someone before inviting him to Thanksgiving? I mean, hypothetically speaking. Also hypothetically, the person being invited might not have anywhere else to go if his job only allows a few days off, and he doesn't want to travel all the way home, which theoretically makes this more of a gesture of goodwill than a premature offer to meet the family, anyway. Right?"

"Definitely. So, I'd say…one date? Hypothetically and theoretically speaking."

"Good answer."

Hope could be a fragile thing and treacherous when dashed, but Eden decided to let it grow. She couldn't see herself with many men, but she could picture herself with Brandon. Maybe this time next year, *she'd* be trying to decide between sit-down or buffet, lilies or white roses.

"Thank you." She returned Nikki's encouraging squeeze. "Now put both hands back on the wheel." They were nearing the Portland off-ramps.

Nikki grinned. "Next stop, PDX."

Nikki slid her compact SUV easily into one of the few available parking spaces on NW Eleventh in Portland's Pearl District. Ryan, an architect, lived with his fiancé in an amazing art deco-style building that always made Eden wish she'd worn seamed stockings.

The women walked along the busy street, enjoying the sunshine, their raincoats left in the car. In true Stumptown fashion, the November weather had turned from gray and chilly to the kind of golden autumn glow that prompted Portlanders to greet each other with, "Beautiful day!"

A barely there breeze tickled the leaves of trees lining the avenue, and the Portland streetcar chortled past as the women made their way toward Ryan's street.

"Olli's been posting wedding tablescapes on Pinterest. They're brilliant," Nikki said excitedly. Ryan, his fiancé and Nikki were both in full wedding prep, and Eden nodded, grateful for the opportunity to speak privately with her big brother while Nik and Olli debated whether peonies were too large for a bouquet.

Nikki stopped abruptly as they reached Bite Me, a bakery that exclusively sold bite-size cookies in more varieties than Baskin Robbins sold ice cream. "We should get a box," Nikki announced, practically salivating at the window. "I hate to arrive empty-handed."

"Ryan and Olli don't expect you to—"

"Shut up." Grabbing Eden's arm, she pulled her toward the door.

Nikki had a clerk layer one of their large Tiffany-blue boxes with a variety of tantalizing cookies, while Eden picked up a smaller box for Barney and Charlene and one for Gideon, too, as a thank-you for caring for her last night. They grabbed a couple of samples (okay, so more than a couple, but the clerk offered) and, still chewing, crossed the street to the elegant building.

"Sometimes I wonder if I should move back to Portland," Nikki said, wagging her head at the dignified luxury of even the hallways in the building. "Look at this style. Plus fabulous food, shopping districts and a latte on every corner."

"We have that in Holliday. On a smaller, homier scale."

"Much smaller. Way homier."

"We have twinkle lights all year round."

"True. I'd miss the twinkle lights. But Portland has Powell's, the world's greatest bookstore."

"You've got me there."

Reaching her brother's door, Eden pressed the bell and heard the faint sound of wheels rolling across hardwood. It had been a few weeks since her last trip to Portland, and Ryan's firm was working on the expansion of a retirement facility on River Road in Milwaukie, so he hadn't been able to get away, either.

The door opened to his smiling face and the energy with which he seemed to vibrate. According to their parents, he'd been on the move since he'd learned how to crawl. An all-star on every athletic team he'd ever joined, Ry had shoulders to rival Brandon's, rock-solid arms and the sculpted-jaw good looks of a guy who could garner positive attention just by blinking.

"Ladies," he greeted as he looked up at them, "You're both gorgeous as ever. And cookies from Bite Me?" The welcoming smile broadened to a grin. "Hey, Ol," he called over his shoulder, "hold the cup of mud, bring on the moo juice!"

Maneuvering his state-of-the-art Küschall wheelchair backward, Ryan opened the door wider to admit them.

"Far be it from me to state the obvious, but you haven't worked in a diner for fifteen years," Eden ribbed her brother. "Do you use the lingo to drive Olli crazy?"

"Yes, he does," Olli agreed, joining them in the entry and squeezing Ryan's shoulder. "Why are we drinking milk like third-graders? I was going to make cappuccinos." Six foot three and lean as a lamppost, Olli stepped forward to give his future sister-in-law a bear hug and plant a kiss on her cheek. When he went to hug Nikki, he noticed the blue box. "Ah, the plot thickens. We're having milk *and cookies*. Or more accurately—" he winked at Eden "—the three of us will be drinking milk while your brother eats his weight in snickerdoodles."

"I got tired of the snickerdoodles two weeks ago. Try to keep up." Ryan arched a brow at Nikki. "Did you happen to get the honey-roasted peanut butter bites? Or the drunken raspberry bars?"

"Plenty of both."

"Of all my sister's friends, you're my favorite."

Nikki put a hand on her chest. "I love that you can be bought."

"With an ease that should shame him, but doesn't," Olli confirmed, adding to Eden, "I'll take the cookies while you stage an intervention. Nikki, want to join me in the kitchen, so we can pretend to pour milk? I want to talk to you about your cake photos on Pinterest. The isomalt butterflies? Gorgeous."

"I know! They're going to be painted in shades of aqua and lavender. I was going to serve petit fours, too, but now I'm thinking of having a cookies-and-milk bar at the reception," Nikki said as she and Olli headed toward the open-concept kitchen. "What do you think? Fun and whimsical or been-there-done-that?"

"It's all in the presentation," Ollison Franklin Mackin IV, artistic director of Theatre Unlimited, assured. Olli was approaching his own wedding like theatre, which appealed to Nikki, who continually looked to him for ideas. "Think of it as a set. Tiers of cookies and milk with a pastel ombré effect to carry over the colors of the butterflies. Come to my office. I'll draw some quick sketches. If you want a cookie bar, you'll have it, and it will be anything but been-there-done-that."

Ryan hitched his head toward the pair as they

abandoned the cookie box on the polished concrete island and headed to Ollison's office.

"He lives for this," Ryan said affectionately. "Come on, let's take all the peanut butter bites before they come back."

The kitchen was set up for Ryan to be perfectly independent, and Eden knew better than to offer her help. Her brother had become a waiter at seventeen, specifically because no one had believed he should try it. Talking his way into a job at a place called The Diner Down Under—accessed via a ramp that led to a restaurant tucked into the basement of a building with concrete floors perfect for wheels—Ryan had proved he could be quick, inventive (he used the shop at their high school to attach a carrying "shelf" over the arms of his chair) and eternally positive.

Maneuvering his chair with one hand this morning, Ry used the other to pour two glasses of milk, which he handed to Eden while he balanced a plate loaded with cookies on his lap and led them back to the light-filled living room. A wall of southeast-facing windows offered a truly enviable view of downtown. As cities went, Portland was pretty fantastic, Eden had to admit. There were too many memories, too much water under the bridge for her to want to move back to the city, but she certainly understood why Ryan had no plans ever to leave.

"Okay, what's up, you bright sunflower? I got

a missed call, but no message." Ryan popped a cookie in his mouth and semi-drained the glass of milk while watching her carefully. "I was kind of looking forward to one of your rambling voice mails."

"I don't ramble."

"'Hi, Ryan, how are you today? I'm fine. Have you ever seen *Monarch of the Glen*, it's so good—I'm thinking of taking up tai chi to relax—do you like rooibos tea—I wish Mom and Dad had given us more direction about dating when we were younger—we should go on a cruise to Alaska. Call me, if you get a chance.'" He raised a brow.

"Well, we should go on a cruise to Alaska."

"Why didn't you leave a message this time?"

"It was too complicated to explain."

"S'plain now, Lucy," he said, his mouth full of raspberry bar. Ry had lost the use of his legs in the same automobile accident that had left Eden with her scars. Back when they were recuperating at home, their dad, a firm believer that laughter could stop wars and heal pestilence, had bought them the complete set of *I Love Lucy* on VHS. She and Ryan had memorized six seasons of Lucy-Ricky dialogue, shooting it back and forth to each other at the dinner table until their mother had pleaded for silence and their father had apologized for bringing the videos home.

Topic number one: with sweaty palms, thudding heart and adrenaline pulsing sickeningly through her veins, she announced, "I'm ready to date again."

Tilting back his head, Ryan tossed a quarter-sized peanut butter cookie into the air, caught it in his mouth and chewed. "'Bout time."

Eden waited. "That's it?" she said. "That's all you've got? Ryan, I'm not talking about dating just for the hell of it. I'm talking about dating, because…" Nerves flying sky-high here. "I want to get married again. Soon." That sounded presumptuous under the circumstances. Also slightly desperate. "Soonish. Soonish rather than laterish. I want to have kids, and I'm not old, certainly—thirty-sixish is not *old*—"

"Man, that's a lot of ishes."

"You know, I think I should start exploring whether it's possible—physically possible—for me to have a baby, and I would like to do that with the support and love of a partner." It occurred to her that she was perched on the edge of the sofa, like a skydiver trying to decide whether to jump. "A partner I'm married to," she clarified. "I've decided that definitively. I want to be married. I've always wanted to be married…well, except for a while after I was married."

"Look at you, rambling in person so I don't have to wait for a voice mail."

Eden gave him the sister glare. "Can you be helpful?"

"Sorry, Ed. Look, I've wanted you to get back on the horse for years, you know that. But while you're sitting there telling me you're ready, you're tense as hell." His tone was not unkind. "Your hands are clenched, you look clammy. You seem more like someone who's afraid of heights getting ready to bungee jump than a beautiful woman about to get back in the dating game."

It was somehow incredibly powerful and also unbearably poignant to hear Ryan refer to her as beautiful. Eden felt tears behind her eyes. "You know why."

"Because you have scars on your otherwise mobile and healthy body?" He waved a hand over his legs. "Not impressed, Ed."

Ryan had not wallowed in self-pity after the accident. Gotten angry, railed over losing the use of his legs, fought the prognosis he would never walk again? Yes, all of that. But he'd rejected self-pity. Unlike her, it should be noted in the interest of keeping it real. By the time he'd left the hospital, Ry had accept that he was paraplegic and had poured his focus into gaining as much autonomy as possible over every area of his life. He'd never tolerated their mother's attempts to baby him "just until you're on your feet again"—a statement that had triggered an avalanche of dark humor that sent their nervous mom to bed for a week. If anyone teared up around him (and let's face it, "star high school running back loses use of his legs in a car accident on the way home from state playoffs" tended to elicit some weeping), Ryan would entertain empathy for about a second and sympathy not at all. If this was life, then he intended to get on with it.

"You sucked up all the resilience in the gene pool," she lamented. "Ry, didn't you ever wonder if someone you loved would love you back? Or whether you'd have to settle? Or if you'd be loved at all? Before Ollison, I mean."

"Of course. But I got most of my dwelling done before high school."

"Explain that, please."

He smiled. "Even before the accident I was filled with self-doubt about whether I'd be loved."

"Okay, that is actually a surprise. You? Mr. football star, baseball star, prom king, high-school success story?"

"*Gay* football, baseball, prom king success story. Queer in Milwaukie, Oregon, in 2000 did not belong in the plus column." Ryan's lively eyes held his sister's. "I came out after the accident, partly because I figured the 'rents would be so relieved I wasn't dead, they'd overlook the part about being gay. I hated the accident— the fact of it, what it did to me, what it did to us all. I was just rebellious enough to begin to truly accept myself, because I figured if life was going to take my legs,

I sure as hell wasn't going to give away anything else that belonged to me."

Eden gazed at her big brother with the admiration she'd always felt for him. "I'm not as self-actualized as you. Mom and Dad must have hired a better therapist for you than they did for me."

"Yeah, I'm sure that's it. So, what are you going to do about it now?"

With the view of the city around her, a city that prized boldness and originality, Eden didn't think *Well, there's this guy, and I'm comparing his behavior to an article to see if he likes me* was a worthy response.

"I met someone."

"And?"

"And that's it so far. I've only met him once. But I really like him."

"Are you waiting for him to ask you out?"

Eden made a scrunchy face. "Maybe."

"In the meantime, you're worrying about what he'll say when he finds out you're not perfect." Ryan wagged his handsome head. "So why don't you ask him out? And no, you don't have to tell him about the scars first. Just be your badass self and see where it goes."

"Because if he really loves me, my looks won't matter?" Eden couldn't help keep the bitterness from her tone.

"Because no matter what happens, you've still got

you. And me and Ollison and Nikki. You'll be fine, Ed. Also, you may date the guy and decide he's not for you. You said yourself you barely know him."

That wasn't exactly what she'd said, but if she discounted newspaper articles and gossip, then it was kind of true.

"How are things going with the landlord from hell?" Ryan asked, looking mournfully at his empty cookie plate.

"Uh, we should probably stop calling him that. I think we may be becoming friends. Or, friendly. It's hard to tell. He's kind of awkward, but also very considerate as it turns out. Kind of warm. Ish."

"Again with the *ish*."

"It's hard to be completely unreserved, because he runs hot and cold."

"Hmm. In a needs-to-be-evaluated-for-sociopathic-tendencies way?" Ryan adopted his protective-big-brother persona—expression dead serious, broad shoulders squared.

"No, he's sane. Just sad, I think."

Ryan watched her closely for a few seconds, then sighed heavily and wagged his handsome head. "Uh-oh."

Chapter Seven

Eden narrowed her eyes at her brother. "What 'uh-oh'?"

"You have that 'I can save him,' overzealous glow." Worry and caution narrowed his hazel eyes.

Couldn't ding him for watching out for her. "No, I don't," she assured. "And he would hate it if he thought I was trying to 'save' him. I just sense he could be happier if he was more connected to the community."

"You're going to connect him?"

"I can help."

"I thought you bug the crap out of him."

"Things change. I think he wants to be friends, but isn't quite ready to let down his guard."

"Why is his guard up to begin with?"

Eden leaned forward, feeling an eagerness that reminded her how much she loved a good mystery. "I don't know. Maybe it's like the Red Sea."

"Excuse me?"

"Sometimes it takes one person to step forward first. Like Nachshon jumping into the Red Sea and then *poof*! The waters part, and you've got yourself a bona fide miracle. And all it took was a little faith."

He smiled. "I'll take your word for that."

She only knew about Nachshon and the Red Sea because their grandma Esther on their mom's side, whom they'd called Bubbie, had offered to send them to Hebrew school when they were young. Ryan had declined, citing interference with his sports practice, but Eden had liked Bubbie Esther, her stories about living in Brooklyn in the 1950s, the perfect crystal dish of candy Bubbie had set out on her battered, ancient coffee table and the yummy soup smells that greeted her when she'd visited Esther's southwest Portland apartment. Their mother and father had thought Hebrew school was overkill, but Bubbie Esther had offered, and Eden had begged to be allowed to go.

Every Wednesday and Sunday after class, Eden would go back to Esther's place, where they would play five-card draw with her neighbors and eat homemade rugelach by the plateful before dinner. Toward the end of every visit, Esther would pull out her knitting. "Good friends are like an afghan. Something you can feel safe with," she would say each time she picked up her needles and got to work. "This afghan is for you, *bubelah*," she'd tell Eden, needles clicking as she worked. "Use it in good health." To this day, Eden could wrap the afghan around her and *feel* the laughter, the good-natured kibbitzing and the comfort of those lovable poker players. That's what Gideon needed: the comfort of people who cared about whether he had an afghan. The reassurance of connection.

"I'll introduce you to Gideon the next time you visit me in Holliday instead of making me come up here all the time, and, yes, I meant for that to be a guilt trip."

"Gee, Mom and Dad really did get me the better therapist."

"Are you and Olli coming to the community Hanukkah party?"

"Miss the chance to see a giant menorah in the middle of Mayberry? Nothing could keep us away."

"Holliday is not Mayberry. We are a hip town."

"You haul in fake snow for winter."

"Only once. And everyone agreed it was too hard to clean up, so it's never going to happen again. Anyway, you can meet Gideon at the menorah lighting."

"I thought he was a hermit."

Eden frowned deliberately. "That was before he made a friend like me. I'm irrepressible."

"Relentless, too."

She tapped her thumb and forefinger together, then quickly quelled the nervous gesture. "You'll be able to meet Brandon there, too. The guy I'm interested in."

That got Ryan's full attention. "I'm looking forward to it."

"Good. I want you to meet him and give me your gut-level opinion." She nodded casually, then added much too fervently, "I know you're going to love him, though. He's so kind and such a compassionate person. He just moved to town this year and already volunteers on two civic committees and organized a youth group."

Ryan laughed at her. "Okay, you *do* live in Mayberry. Your love interest is Sheriff Andy Taylor, he has a son named Opie who's going to grow up to be Ron Howard, and Aunt Bea is baking the wedding cake."

With her expression, Eden gave him the equivalent of her middle finger. "You aren't the only person in this family allowed to fall madly in love, Rye Bread."

"No, but at least I waited until after the first date."

"Details." She waved away his protest, then smiled. "I think he really is perfect for me, Ry."

Her big brother's face softened. "Olli and I will be there for Hanukkah. I want to meet the man who inspired my sister to unlock her heart."

Opening the car door after Nikki pulled to the curb in front of Eden's half of the duplex much later that evening, Eden saw that she'd forgotten to leave a light on at her place. The living room at Gideon's, however, was ablaze.

"Thanks for driving. I had fun," she told Nikki as she exited the car with her purse and the box of cookies she'd picked up at Bite Me.

Nikki leaned forward. "I had a great time, and I got some wonderful ideas from Olli. Promise we'll still have carbohydrate Saturdays and all-day trips to Portland after I'm married."

"*I* promise. It'll be up to you. Just don't expect me ever to eat keto bagels, because there shouldn't be any such thing."

With her full lips curving, Nikki confessed, "I picture our get-togethers staying husband-free and carbo-heavy."

"Now you're talkin'. See you soon." Shutting the door, Eden waved her friend off and waited until the taillights rounded the corner before she turned toward her own walkway.

Going home meant spending the rest of the evening alone, which ought to be welcome after a day full of other people, but Eden was restless. Being with the blissfully engaged fueled her anticipation, yet roused her insecurities as well.

What Nikki didn't know—nor did Ryan or anyone else for that matter—was that Eden had tried to have another relationship after Josh left.

Oh yes. She hadn't always been celibate and self-protective and closed off. There'd been a period, a short one, during which she'd thought she'd jump back into the dating pool. Working in the library of a large corporate law firm in Portland, she'd gotten to know one of the attorneys well. Very well.

She'd gone into the relationship with Lucas telling herself she was purposefully rebounding, albeit almost a year after Josh had left. She was going to have some fun (and some sex) and learn to take life a lot less seriously. Josh had been her first boyfriend, and when he'd stayed with her after the accident, she'd been grateful, so grateful she'd never questioned whether their sex life had left something (a lot) to be desired.

Deciding to be worldly and up-front with Lucas, she'd told him about the accident and its impact without even being self-deprecating. He'd told her she was gorgeous, that a few scars couldn't change that. "Oh, it's more than a few," she'd quipped, breezy as hell, trying to convey the casual self-acceptance she'd practiced for weeks.

Unfortunately, practiced sophistication had been no match for the reality of actually making love with someone new.

Scratch that. She had *tried* to make love with someone new. The act had not been successfully completed. In fact, one could term it a complete frigging disaster. Lucas's message that Eden was beautiful, that no scar could change that, had not, unfortunately, registered with his body. Lucas may have wanted to have sex with her; his penis hadn't. It was hard to forget a thing like that.

The experience had been so traumatic she defied anyone in a similar situation not to grab her phone immediately and ask, "Siri, how do I join an abbey?"

Outside the duplex, a lone streetlamp shined a spotlight on a red-hued maple, its five-pointed leaves jitterbugging in the snappy night breeze. It would be a fine time to curl into the arms of the man beside you on the sofa while the fire warmed your faces. Too bad the only male on her sofa was a cat with attachment issues.

Looking up the street, she contemplated a walk. The moon and stars were out this evening in a sky much clearer than her cloudy thoughts. But there was no one else outside, nobody to stop and blab with, nothing to distract her from the storm brewing in her mind. Nothing except the lights on at Gideon's.

Without giving herself time to rethink the move, Eden headed across the lawn she shared with her landlord, the box of cookies she'd bought for him in the crook of her arm. Still ten feet away from his apartment, she heard music. Opera.

A rhododendron partially but not completely— blocked a window that was a mirror image of hers, and Eden could see the man himself standing in profile in the middle of his living room. She should have gone straight to the door and rung the bell at that point. But she didn't. Nope. Pushing aside thin, leaf-covered branches, she edged behind the rhodie, crouching so that she remained out of sight.

There wasn't much to see in the living room, which was depressingly Spartan, the walls still white, as per the previous landlord's rental agreement. (Eden had painted her walls Matcha Latte the moment she'd heard the duplex was changing hands.) Gideon had no decoration on the walls, and the furniture looked like something he'd found on sale at the local big-box store. Nothing at all suggested *home*, except for a wall unit that held a turntable—the old-fashioned kind that was making a comeback—a CD player, speakers and an extensive collection of albums and CDs. He did things the old-fashioned way, Gideon did.

The music appeared to be affecting him deeply. He stood perfectly still, his head bent forward, a glass of amber liquid in one hand, the other hand buried in his pants pocket. The music must have been turned up as high as possible, because she could clearly hear *Rigoletto*'s "All'onda, all'onda."

Holy cannoli. He was listening to the gut-wrenching scene in which Rigoletto sings to his dying daughter, Gilda. She'd seen it performed not that long ago, because Ryan and Ollison had season tickets to Portland Opera and passed them to her when they couldn't attend. Cheerful stuff, that *Rigoletto*. Treachery, betrayal, sacrifice and threats rolled into two-and-a-half hours of serious fun. If that was the mood Gideon was in, perhaps it would be better to—

No time to finish that thought.

As Rigoletto's tragic baritone poured out all the anguish and remorse a man could possess, Gideon raised the arm holding his drink and hurled the glass against the far wall.

Eden yelped, even though the glass was thrown away from her. Sheer amazement made her heart pound. The Dark Lord of the Duplex was full of surprises. When he turned to smack the CD player to Off, her knees hit the dirt as she ducked. Good thing she'd worn pants today. She very cautiously poked her head up above the sill again.

Amber liquid stained the white wall on the opposite side of the room, and broken glass littered the wood floor, but Gideon seemed either not to realize the damage or not to care. Returning his back to her, he lowered his head once more, his shoulders so tense they all but swallowed his neck. His pain was so palpable and so private that the entire core of Eden's body throbbed in aching unity.

Neither the shrubs nor the cover of evening (nor the convenient lapse of integrity that allowed her to spy on him in the first place) could make her comfortable continuing to invade Gideon's privacy, so she did the dignified thing. Hiking her coat out of the way and attempting to ignore the soil she was grinding into her new Theory Max C pants, she crawled on her hands and knees until she was clear of the window, then stood up and crouch-walked across his lawn.

Ohhhhkay, at least now she'd have someone besides herself to think about tonight. What could have made Gideon, a man who made starfish seem impetuous, erupt like that? He was a mystery.

And if she were being honest with herself, one she would like to start unraveling.

Maybe they wouldn't watch *The Crown* together, after all. *Dr. Who* seemed like a better choice.

Digging into her purse, Eden pulled out her house keys and shivered a little inside her coat as she opened her door. Gideon had looked so alone. A wash of loneliness assailed her in response.

She'd lived without a special man in her life for years, and she'd been fine. *Fine.* The absence of a partner wasn't what bothered her; it was the treacherous possibility of *more* that was biting her on the ass.

Maybe she should be grateful for friends and leave it at that. Life was certainly simpler when you stopped trying to change the situations—and people—you couldn't. (Sorry for not embracing that concept a couple of decades ago, Oprah.) She would focus on her book group, on Barney and Charlene, and maybe she'd start a movie club. Business as usual; inertia was highly underrated.

Plan of action for rest of the evening: watch *Thelma and Louise* and give herself a face mask while drinking mint tea with a splash—just a splash—of white rum and lemon. Never let it be said that a woman could not enjoy her life free from the complications of a Y chromosome.

Her plan held for as long as it took her to reach her front porch, where she saw an arrangement of flowers—yellow roses, pink ranunculus and two winter tulips emerging from a ceramic pot someone had placed atop the small, aqua-painted bistro table on her porch.

Flowers! Lovely, *hopeful* flowers. Like a hummingbird, her heart seemed to flit backward, forward and upside down. She didn't even wait to go inside; setting her purse and cookie box on the table, she reached for the small envelope tucked between the blooms. The note inside was handwritten.

She read it twice, then plopped onto the little chair she sometimes sat in to drink coffee in the morning and watch the neighborhood come alive. A smile spread slowly across her lips. Now *she* was coming alive. *Damn.* Just when she told herself it was time to accept life the way it was, it went ahead and changed. *Everything* changed.

Reading the note again, she drummed her feet on the porch in sheer happiness, then dug into her purse to find her phone and make a call. An elated sigh escaped as she lifted the phone to her ear.

"Nik," she exclaimed as her friend picked up, "you're not going to believe what happened."

Chapter Eight

Gideon picked up shards of glass without gloves, aware that accidentally nicking himself would be one more punishment he thought he deserved. He'd had enough therapy to realize that much, anyway.

Pieces of the broken tumbler clinked as if toasting each other when he dropped them into the trash can he'd brought to the living room. He'd have to mop the hardwood floor, too.

The aroma of whiskey assaulted his nostrils. He'd never gotten the hang of drowning his feelings in alcohol, though he'd certainly given it a good try. Unable to drown his feelings, he'd felt as if *he* were drowning—slowly, day by day. Every attempt to help seemed to push him lower. When it had gotten harder and harder to breathe, he'd decided to move to this unlikely town, away from everyone who'd been trying to save him.

By then he'd figured out that people live together but die alone. He'd decided to be alone here, in Holliday, going through the motions, marking off the days. But then he'd met Eden, with her dramatic wardrobe and her constant chatter. Her unquenchable *aliveness*. Who sat outside in the rain to talk on the phone? She did, under strings of lights, with music playing and her hair glistening with raindrops. Who brought makeup and strands of gaudy beads to an elderly stroke victim so she could "feel glamorous" even if all she could do at the time was sit up in bed? Eden did, and Charlene and Barney adored her for it. Eden was breath and vitality, enthusiasm and hope.

He hated hope.

"Dumned fool idiot." Brushing the rest of the shards into a dustpan, he dumped the mess into the trash. He was caught in a tug-of-war between his willingness to let himself sink toward the cold, dark bottom of the ocean and an unexpected pull toward Eden, who was the sun he could see shining above the surface.

It was quieter, safer at the bottom, but tonight the pull toward Eden won. Gideon strode toward his front door, hesitating as he reached for the knob even though he knew he would turn it sooner or later.

Outside, the crisp night air cooled his hot face. He turned toward her side of the duplex and started walking. The porch light he'd noticed earlier was still on, but now the sound of feminine laughter broke the silence. Halfway between their two units, he stopped and listened.

"I told you he's perfect." Filled with teasing, Eden's voice conveyed the effervescence he was used to hearing when she talked to her friends. "He'll send me ranunculus for every anniversary, I bet. And I will, of course, plant them in the garden until we have fifty years' worth of flowers." Her laughter sounded like a waterfall. "Well, I plan on having a big yard. More room for kids."

She kept talking, her feet swinging merrily, a small pot of bright flowers on a table beside her. He'd seen her seated by that table on weekend mornings, drinking coffee and chatting with neighbors who walked by.

Damned fool idiot. Him, not her.

Hoping like hell she wouldn't notice him, Gideon turned and walked swiftly back to his apartment, lowered the shades and got a mop to clean the mess he'd made in the house since he couldn't clean up the mess he'd made of his life.

Eden was a woman falling in love, looking toward a future filled with promise. Maybe she'd have kids. Probably she'd have kids. That was not the direction in which his life was headed. It had been temporary insanity to want—

Well. Never mind what he'd wanted. He had two cardinal rules for survival:

1. Keep your distance.
2. Keep your secrets.

He knew what people thought of him: he was cold, remote, unfeeling. They didn't realize that *feelings* were the anchor that had dragged him down to begin with. If he had any hope of treading water, he needed to stick to his rules. Especially with Eden.

Eden awoke to a sound she knew she did not like even though her sleepy brain had yet to identify the source. Blinking groggily, she glanced around and saw Malfoy perched atop the end table, chewing on a ranunculus.

"Hey, leave my flowers alone!" Popping up, she shooed the wiry feline away from her gift. The cat hissed loudly, then jumped to the floor, where he took a moment to attend to some personal hygiene.

The room was still gray with morning shadows. What time was it, anyway? Eden reached for her phone. Six forty-seven on a Sunday morning. "You are a very bad cat," she scolded, but her heart wasn't in the rebuke. Not today. Not with a surprise flower arrangement and card sitting so nearby!

*Sure hope you're feeling better. If there's any-
thing I can do, please call.*

She smiled, burrowing happily beneath the covers. She had flowers. Flowers and a card. With a
heart-eye emoji. And Brandon's phone number.

Hugging her pillow, she kicked her feet against
the mattress, thoroughly enjoying the feeling of
being fourteen again. 'Bout time she woke up
looking forward to something more exciting than
breakfast.

When a thumping sound interrupted the happy
buzz of her thoughts, Eden pushed down the covers and searched the shadowed room for Malfoy.
"Whatever poorly behaved thing you're doing, stop
immediately." But Malfoy was sitting in the middle
of the room, still licking.

Sitting all the way up, she realized someone
was knocking on her front door. Before seven in
the morning on a Sunday? Sighing, she swung her
legs over the side of the bed. The cat would want
his morning binge now, anyway. Picking up her
flowers, she carried them with her as she trudged
to the living room. No one who knew her would
expect a hearty welcome—or any welcome at all—
at oh-dark-thirty on a Sunday morning, though
possibly it was Cooper Deagan, who was eighty-
two and sweet as all get-out, but occasionally mis-
placed his prosthetic leg and rang doorbells at all
hours to ask if anyone had seen it. She padded to

the living room window, where she flicked the blinds and peered out onto the porch.

It wasn't Cooper.

Without hesitation, she turned the dead bolt and swung the door open. "Hi! How are you? Is everything okay? Are you okay? You look sweaty."

"I went for a run." Gideon stood on her porch, appearing not only sweaty but also tired, as if he hadn't slept.

Memory of last night's scene in his living room flooded back. She reached for his arm, pulling him across the threshold. "Come in. I'm glad you dropped by. You're welcome anytime you want to come over and gab. That's what friends are for, right?" And after what she saw last night, he definitely needed a friend.

Brandon's flowers had distracted her; she hadn't given nearly enough time to unraveling the mystery of Gideon's painful outburst. "Are you hungry? I can make breakfast. Well," she amended before he got his hopes up. "I can *pour* breakfast into bowls. I have an excellent cereal assortment. My tastes extend way beyond Fruity Pebbles."

"I'm not here for breakfast." Looking bemused and uncomfortable, he responded awkwardly. "Or for…gabbing." Typical Gideon.

"Okay. If you're not interested in coffee, Peanut Butter Cap'N Crunch or riveting conversation, why are you here?" She tried to say it nicely, but honestly, what was it going to take?

"I'm here strictly in my capacity as your land-lord."

Oh, brother. When he began to sound like con-stipated *Downton Abbey,* her empathy fled, and she felt like throttling him. "I hate to sound judgy," she said, "but some people sleep in on Sunday mornings. I'm one of them. So unless you've mis-placed a prosthetic leg, maybe you should come back later."

"Prosthetic leg? Why would I have—"

"Never mind. Why are you here?"

"We appear to have a prowler," he explained.

That caught her off guard. "A prowler? In Hol-liday?"

"On this property."

"Oh, my gosh." Eden shivered, wrapping her arms around her waist.

"I'll be installing a home security system. Of course, you're welcome to select your own if you prefer and have it installed at my expense. It's a sound investment and a write-off for me."

She tried not to roll her eyes. Was this really the same person who had dinner with her? "You know, you run hot and cold more than my shower."

"Is there something wrong with your water heater? You should have spoken up sooner."

"There's nothing wrong with the water heater."

"You just said—"

"Gideon, it was just an expression. I have a question, though. Why did you buy a duplex instead of, say, a single-family dwelling surrounded by electrified wire?"

He ran a finger around the crew-style collar of his sweatshirt, tugging as if the loose neckline was as restrictive as a starched shirt. "The landlord-renter relationship isn't meant to be personal. It's efficient. Functional. It should be service-based."

"You're impossible, you know that? I'm trying to be friends with you, but it's like trying to get a squirrel to relax."

Tension hardened his jawline, and she felt instant remorse. Gideon was intelligent and had proved on Friday night that inside the ice shell lurked a warm, appealing, even humorous man. Damn it, she owed him another apology. She ought to be patient and slowly tease the trust out of him.

"Gideon," she tried again, her voice softer and more placating, "listen—" She'd lost his attention.

"What is that?" Brushing past her suddenly, he headed for the short counter that divided the kitchen from the dining area, stopping with his back to her.

Before she could figure out what he was talking about, he made a half turn back to her and repeated, "What is that?"

The change in his demeanor—stormy gray eyes

in an ashen face—called her attention toward the kitchen. There wasn't much to see. Limited counter space (really ought to talk to the landlord about that), necessitated small and few appliances. The only apparatus on her counter were a Keurig and a single-serving-size high-speed blender for smoothies. Basic single-woman stuff.

"What is what?" she asked.

Gideon's chest rose with a sharp, angry intake of breath. In two strides he was at the peninsula dividing the rooms. Sweeping a small blue box up from the counter, he held it out. "This."

"Cookies. From Bite Me in the Pearl." She shook her head. What was the problem? "Charlene loves the Lemon-Lemon bites, so I picked up a box for her and Barney when I was in Portland yesterday. I got one for you, too." She looked around for the second box. "Where did I—" A prickle of unease crawled along her skin.

"I went for a jog," Gideon said, his voice tight. "Mrs. Gurney's beagle dug under her fence again. I found it rooting around behind the rhododendron in front of my living room window." He waited, and somehow his icy gray eyes burned.

Oh, no. Oh, no, no, no. It couldn't be... "That dog is a rascal," she said, apropos of nothing, just buying some time while her mind resisted the proof in front of her. "Did you take him home?"

"He was chewing on a box of cookies." For a

moment, there was only heavy breathing (hers) and cold stony silence (his). Gideon looked at the box in his hand, then slowly replaced it on the counter. "Yeah, I took him home. He'd eaten almost an entire box of cookies. You were spying on me," he said, his quiet conclusion much more awful than a furious accusation.

"I wasn't spying," she denied, "I was—" *Spying.* "The cookies were for you." *Because a spoonful of sugar makes the egregious invasion of someone's privacy go down in the most delightful way.* "Gideon, I wasn't…" His brows lowered like a guillotine, so she stopped short of another denial. "All right. I was. I mean I wasn't 'spying' exactly, it was more like…" She began to perspire. "Wow, where's a thesaurus when you need one? How can I describe this accurately? I was watching you in an uninvited way." She watched his expression. Okay, not better. "I was going to ring your doorbell to give you the cookies, and then I realized, 'Hey, wait a minute, Gideon does not seem like the type to enjoy drop-in company in the evening.'"

"But I do seem like the type to enjoy stalking?"

Eden drew a sharp breath. "Hey, I definitely was not stalking. Also, in my defense, your curtains were open."

"There's a rhododendron the size of a refrigerator in front of that window."

Hot and sickening, embarrassment crawled

through her veins. They both knew she'd had to squeeze behind the rhodie to get a good view. "Okay, yes, I totally invaded your privacy. I saw your lights on, and I really was going to give you the cookies, but then I heard the music—I mean, c'mon, *Rigoletto*?—and I was curious."

"Curiosity gives you the right to pry into my life?"

"No. It doesn't. I guess nothing gives me that right, and you certainly haven't invited me, but I know pain when I see it."

"Pain. You think you know pain." It was a challenge.

"Yes. I do. And I know it shouldn't be carried alone." He remained stonily silent, so she continued. "So, the reason I was looking in your window is I've noticed that since you moved to Holliday… You're sort of on the outside looking in. And I get that. I truly do. For a lot of my life I've felt different from other people. I looked in your window, because I guess I just felt as if I…recognized you."

Eden realized she was perspiring. For perhaps the first time in her adult life, she realized she might be on the brink of a genuine connection with a man. As if all her scars were clearly visible, and it didn't matter. Was it her imagination, or did Gideon's sharply angled face seem less severe? Everyone wanted to be understood by at least one other human being, didn't they? Every life needed a witness.

Their eyes remained locked for three more strong heartbeats. She smiled at him.

Gideon's chest rose on a deep inhalation. "We're not alike. You don't know me." His tone was spiritless, but final. "You don't know me at all." Then he turned, opened the door and walked out.

The silence was deafening.

Wait a minute. Having lost count of the times Gideon had rejected her overtures of friendship, Eden figured she probably shouldn't be surprised by one more slight, yet she was. She'd admitted her fault. She'd been open. Empathetic, even. She'd been damned genuine. And he walked out without a word?

Yanking the door open, she revved up to give him a piece of her mind, but instantly decided against it and slammed the door shut again. Why should she care? Why? She didn't need more problems in her life. She had flowers from someone who seemed happy and easygoing. Pressing her back against the front door, she closed her eyes and imagined being with Brandon, feeling as if she had no scars, no angst, no loneliness. It felt good. It was what she wanted. She wasn't going to let a cranky, isolated man get in the way of that. Gideon was a ship passing in her night.

Wrapping her arms around herself, Eden shivered even though it was perfectly warm in the apartment. She had closed the door on Gideon so many times after a confrontation, thinking *good riddance!* and it had felt satisfying. This time there was no relief. This time, Gideon's exit felt depressingly final.

Eden dug *Major Pettigrew's Last Stand* from the large bag she always brought with her to Charlene's. "Do you want to see if Major Pettigrew is making any progress with Mrs. Ali?" she asked. "I'll make mint tea to go with the cookies."

Sun had broken through the clouds to turn the gray day into a palette of blue and gold and burnt orange. Perfect for tea, cookies and a British romance.

Charlene was out of bed and seated in the living room on this Sunday, albeit in her wheelchair, with Eden seated on the sofa. Barney had headed to work a few minutes ago, leaving Eden in charge of making Charlene's Sunday as enjoyable as possible. Eden rose now with the intention of setting up a proper tea, but Charlene reached for her arm, hand quivering. "Not…now. Want…to…talk. Sit."

Charlene rarely wanted to converse these days due to the slowness of her speech. Eden sat again instantly, waiting as Charlene worked to form her words.

"Barney…takes…good…care…of…me. Always… not…just…now."

Eden nodded. "I know. You've always taken wonderful care of him, too."

"We've…had…good…life," Charlene continued. "Simple…and…good." She paused, her thin brows drawing together. "Don't…let… Barney…" There was a longer hesitation as she seemed to search for the word she wanted. "…mope. When… I'm…gone. He…has…to…keep…going. That's… important."

Eden felt as if she'd been shocked with ice water. She may have feared for Charlene's life in the very beginning of her health crisis, but not since. Scooting forward on the sofa cushion, she put her hand on her friend's knee and spoke adamantly. "You are going to be fine. You're getting stronger. You were super healthy before this happened, and you've got plenty of years left. You're not going anywhere, young lady. Besides, you still have to teach me how to bake challah. Remember? You told me a few years ago that every bride needs to know how to make a great challah."

"You…never…wanted…to…learn."

"Well, that was before."

Charlene's sea-blue eyes began to sparkle, ageless and undimmed by her health struggles in this moment. Perceptive as ever, she tilted her head. "Change...your...mind...about...bread? Or...marriage?"

Quite a while ago Eden had shared with Charlene that she'd been married once and wasn't inclined to revisit the institution. She hadn't gone into detail, and Charlene hadn't pried, but clearly her memory was sharp as always. Eden shrugged, offering a smile. "Maybe both."

As limited as her facial muscles were, Charlene managed to convey her surprise and pleasure.

"I'm a horrible cook," Eden reminded her friend, though apparently the prompt was unnecessary.

"I...know," Charlene agreed darkly, no doubt remembering the brisket Eden had attempted once when she'd invited the Gleasons to dinner at her place. She'd cooked the hapless cut of meat until it resembled charred wood. Utterly inedible. The mashed potato side hadn't been any better as no one had told her that putting potatoes in a blender rendered them gummy and gross.

"Teaching me to braid a challah could take years," Eden warned. "So you'd better be prepared to stick around."

"Okay," Charlene agreed with more enthusiasm than Eden had witnessed in her friend in some time. "Let's...go." She nodded her head toward the kitchen.

"Now?"

"With...you? No...time...to...waste."

Eden laughed. Baking was *so* not her forte, but color bloomed in Charlene's cheeks. If a stint in her beloved kitchen made her happy, Eden could handle it for an hour or two.

"Okay, off we go." She moved behind Charlene's chair and grasped the handles. "I hope the bread turns out better than the brisket."

"Couldn't...be...any...worse," the older woman quipped.

"Oh, cruel!"

As they rolled through the dining room, Charlene added, "Remember...don't...let...him...mope."

Thirty minutes later, Eden was certain of two things:

One: Charlene was incredibly strong-willed.

And, two: bread baking was only slightly easier than college calculus. Eden's hands looked like those of the Creature from the Black Lagoon. Globs of sticky challah dough clung to every finger and both palms.

"What am I doing wrong?!" she asked Charlene for the umpteenth time.

"Pan...ick...ing," Charlene said succinctly and not without a bit of asperity. "Re-lax. The... dough...can...feel...your...fear."

The dough felt her fear? Could it feel her wanting to throw it against the wall?

It seemed they'd been mixing and stirring and "proofing" and whatever the heck else you did to get all this gunk to morph into a loaf of something edible for, oh, ever. Eden had accepted a long time ago that culinary ability was not in her DNA. Never had been, though she'd done her best to fake it with Josh. He'd had the taste buds of a nine-year-old; it hadn't been hard to please him at the dinner table. Still, she wanted to be able to invite the next man she dated over for a good meal. A real meal, not something she bought in the grocery section of a big-box store and nuked at home. But all this mess!

"Maybe I should start with something easier. You know, a salad."

"Keep…kneading. Add…flour."

Sighing, Eden pushed the mound of dough to the side, sprinkled the marble countertop with flour— "just two teaspoons!"—the way Charlene had told her, then plopped the dough back into the middle of it and shoved the heel of her palm into the center. *Push-fold-turn, push-fold-turn.* Trying to speed the process, she pretended she was performing CPR on the Pillsbury Doughboy. *Stayin' alive, stayin' alive, a-ha-ha-ha—*

"Too…fast!" Charlene reproved. "Re…lax."

"Sorry." About ten thousand minutes later, the heathen dough was resting comfortably in an oiled bowl while Charlene watched *Bridgerton* in the living room. Eden spent a good half hour cleaning the kitchen, after which she tried to pluck dough out of her hair and, inexplicably, her watch.

"Bread dough should be part of every nation's military arsenal. Safer than weapons of mass destruction and less expensive. Just dump it over enemy forces and wait for them to clean their way out," she called to Charlene.

"Ha! Nuclear…dough," her friend agreed.

The doorbell rang.

"I'll get that, then we can binge on *Bridgerton* and drink mocktails in the afternoon until the dough doubles or quadruples or divides itself like an amoeba or whatever it's supposed to do."

Dish towel in hand, she scrubbed at the dough clinging to the front of the apron Charlene loaned her

"I think I know why girls were taught to make challah before they got married," Eden said as she approached the door, commenting on what Charlene had told her the first time she'd broached the idea of teaching Eden to bake. "They're so busy kneading dough, they don't have time to fool around with boys." Charlene's crackling laugh filled the living room. "Which is actually the opposite of what I'm looking for," Eden added, enjoying the lighter mood they'd started in the kitchen. She opened the Gleasons' front door.

"Hi," she sang, then sucked in a breath at the sight of the man on the porch.

His brown hair shot with glittery gold, eyes like a June sky, Brandon Buchanan grinned back at her. "Well, hello. I wasn't expecting to see you here."

"Neither was I," she said too breathlessly. "Expecting you, I mean."

"I'm glad, though." His teeth were as white as a wedding gown.

He. Was. Glad. "Thank you for the flowers." Gratitude whooshed out on a shaky breath.

"You got them. Good! I hope you're feeling better. You look better."

"Oh, I am. I'm fine. Never been better," she assured. No time like the present to make a second first impression.

She stared at him too long. "Come in," she said to break the silence.

Stepping aside, she tried to calm her racing thoughts as he walked past. Holy cow, he smelled as good as before, an aphrodisiac of pheromones, soap and a spicy aftershave. Now that she was standing on the ground instead of atop a stool, she could confirm that he was as tall and Atlas-like as his photos suggested.

Brandon walked directly to Charlene, seating himself in a nearby chair and leaning forward, elbows on his knees as he focused all his attention on Charlene. "It's great to see you again, Mrs. G. Did Barney tell you I'd be coming over today to build a stronger ramp out front? That way you can get in and out of the house more easily."

Her heart quivered like a bow after the arrow had been shot. Could he be any more perfect? When they were married, they would work side by side to help people around town.

"Why don't I get us something to drink?" she offered before she began drooling. "Brandon, what would you like? Something cold, something warm?" *Something as hot as you are?* "I could make a pot of coffee."

"She…bakes…too." Charlene's impish eyes told Eden she had figured out that Brandon was the reason for her sudden interest in baking.

He twisted to look up at her, his expression warm and genuine. "I like to bake, too."

"Do you?"

"Yeah."

"Eden…bakes…bread," Charlene told him.

"No kidding? Bread is my favorite. Any kind."

"You should have some, then."

Brandon looked from her to Charlene, smiling his big, happy Brandon smile. "I knew this was going to be a great day."

His peanut-butter-cup eyes melted her with their

sweetness. This was what she wanted, this…feeling of elation. He was so easy. "Me, too," she replied. "Me, too."

Chapter Nine

"This…is…better…than… *The… Bachelor*," Charlene said, her wheelchair facing the living room window, which afforded a clear view of the porch, where the construction of a better, stronger ramp was in progress.

Eden sat on her knees in a comfy chair next to Charlene. She'd adjusted the furniture to give them both a clear view of the porch and front yard while being far enough away from the window so they couldn't be seen ogling.

"We're not 'spying,'" she reminded Charlene, "because this is your house."

"That's…right."

"We can look in any direction we want while we talk. Sometimes I look at the fireplace." She demonstrated. "Sometimes I look out the window. We're minding our own business."

"Yes." Charlene nodded at Eden before returning her attention to the show outside. "Take...off... your...shirt!" she called out as loudly as she could manage, which probably wasn't loud enough to be heard outside, but Eden shushed her anyway as they dissolved into giggles.

"I never should have agreed to the wine spritzers."

Charlene had decided they required something more exciting than a mocktail for today's live-and-in-person episode of *Yard Crashers*. After checking with Barney, Eden had agreed to the spritzers. Apparently, Gideon had okayed infrequent small amounts of alcohol now that Charlene was a few months away from the stroke. As soon as Eden reflected on that, she thought of Gideon throwing his glass against the wall and a surge of... something—she didn't even know what—made her want once again to talk to him, to draw him out. *Really dumb.*

She and Charlene were enjoyably ogling Brandon, and that was fulfilling enough for anyone. He'd been joined by two of his students from the high school—a girl named Claire, who wore a Portland Pickles baseball cap from which two dark blond braids emerged, and a boy named Jude, who took frequent phone breaks. Brandon put a stop to that by confiscating the cell and reminding Jude that a passing grade in woodworking and community service credits depended on his participation today. Claire and Jude were, apparently, in need of interventions at school, and Brandon had stepped up to give them something constructive to do on the weekends.

"He's kind of perfect, isn't he?" Eden said, or, more accurately, *sighed* as she stared out the window.

"He…has…charm," Charlene commented.

"Exactly. He's charming. Brandon gets along with everyone."

"Very…social. I…can…see…that." Charlene's speech was still slow, but she wasn't struggling for words nearly as much. Eden complimented her on her progress.

"Getting…lots…of…help. Doc… Gideon… is…a…mensch."

"A mensch." Eden pondered that. She'd have used the word to describe Brandon for his community service work, but not necessarily to tag Gideon. Especially not after this morning's ice shower. To her knowledge, Gideon dropped by the Gleason's once a week to take blood pressure and do a med check. That's all. Honestly, his agreeing to that much surprised her, because he'd let it be known that house calls were not a service he provided. "Gideon can be kind of moody. I think he has a lot of baggage. Emotional baggage."

Charlene shrugged. "No…baggage…means… you…never…traveled."

Eden offered a non-committal *hmm*. Since meeting him, she'd wondered where Gideon had "traveled," but she was tired of butting her head against a brick wall. Returning to the much more enjoyable topic of Brandon, she commented on his Alpine shoulders. That was a much simpler topic than Gideon. Brandon had removed the red-and-blue plaid shirt in which he'd arrived, opting to work in only a T-shirt despite the gathering clouds.

"Take…it…off!" Charlene called again just for fun, and Eden clapped her hands as she laughed. Compared with the prior few months, Charlene was downright giddy.

"Make…iced…tea," she said.

"You want iced tea? Looks like it's getting pretty cold out again."

"Not…for…us…dummy." Charlene stabbed a finger toward the window. "For…them."

"Oh, right!"

Fifteen minutes later, Eden was on the porch, setting a small outdoor table with glasses of sweet tea and the packaged cookies she'd found in the Gleasons' cupboard. Being around Brandon made her so nervous, her armpits were damp. Nervously, she smoothed the legs of her palazzo pants—camel colored, high waisted, wide legged. Her hair, still dyed a mink brown, was pulled back into a simple ponytail, and her makeup was subdued compared with her usual dramatic application of shadow and eyeliner.

"Thanks for this," Brandon beamed at her as he took a glass of tea. *Beamed.*

"Of course. You've all been working hard. Can you sit a minute?" She gestured to the porch swing. Awkwardly. Could he see her sweating? She had to quell the urge to pluck at her turtleneck.

"Sure. We're due for a break. Take ten, dudes," he told the kids, who took their tea and cookies to the front yard. Brandon nabbed two Nutter Butters and sat beside Eden on the swing, making it rock gently.

Once his students were immersed in the wonders of their cell phones, Brandon ventured, "You know, I've only lived here a few months now—"

Six, Brandon, but who's counting?

"—and I'm not familiar yet with all the local hiking trails. I've heard Silver Falls is nice."

"It is." Her flirtation skills were so rusty she wasn't sure what to say next. He seemed to be waiting for more commentary on Silver Falls, so she went into Tourist Info mode. "There are walking loops of varying distances. If you want a longer hike, the Trail of Ten Falls will take you past ten waterfalls. You can walk behind some of them. Great photo ops."

He nodded. "Sounds pretty."

"Definitely. Silver Falls is—" *romantic, magical, a great place to kiss* "—very beautiful."

"Is there a good place to stop by for breakfast first?"

"Yes." It occurred to Eden that he might not be planning to hike and grab breakfast alone. Jealousy swooped in, even if he was only going with a friend. She liked to hike. "Silverton has some good cafés," she added, aware he was waiting for her to answer.

"Which do you think is the best?"

"I don't really know," she mumbled.

"Which has the best coffee?"

Oh, for crying out loud, Yelp it. Maybe she wasn't cut out for romance, after all. Maybe she was the female Gideon, broken by inner demons and destined to become acerbic and own a nasty cat that would become her only companion. She sighed. "Main Street Bistro is good."

"Main Street Bistro it is, then."

"Swell."

"How about next Sunday?"

"Dude, that was so lame." Jude looked up from his phone and laughed along with Claire, who added, "I'm making a TikTok of this. My brother's, like, an eighth-grader, and he has more moves than you do, Mr. Buchanan."

Eden's heart boomed in her chest. Had he just asked her out?

Brandon grinned. "It probably was lame. I'm out of practice."

What the hell… It was really happening. She was being asked out by the sweetest guy in town. "It wasn't lame," she quickly assured.

"Yeah, it was," Jude said.

"I'm fine with lame. I like lame. I'm lame." She added a bobblehead nod.

Claire groaned. "Oh, man, I thought getting older would make me cooler. Another dream broken."

Brandon laughed, then winked at Eden, and suddenly the sun was shining, birds sang, daffodils bloomed. It may have been winter in Oregon, but in Eden's heart it was spring. She was not going to be an old woman duking it out for leftover pad thai with a cranky cat, after all. When she was eighty, she was going to dance in the living room with a man who thought she was still sexy.

"So… Sunday?" he asked.

Her whole body tingled. "Definitely."

Approximately an hour and a half after she went back inside, the Gleasons' bungalow smelled like a bakery. Charlene had coached Eden through kneading the dough for a second time, dividing it in half, then cutting each half into thirds as evenly as she could. Next, Charlene told her to roll the six pieces into smooth, equally sized ropes. That was the idea, anyway. Eden's ropes looked like arthritic snakes. The trickiest part of all was braiding three of the knobby strips together without stretching them to jump-rope length, then repeating the process with the other strips.

The frustration seemed to be worth it in the end. By the time the bread was baked and the table set with a crock of butter, a tall wedge of English cheddar and a pitcher of grape juice, Eden felt drained, but proud of herself. Sitting center table in a place of honor, the loaves of challah were large, golden and, as far as she could tell, perfect. As she called everyone in from the front yard, she could *almost* understand why baking the breads was better than buying them in the store.

"I haven't smelled anything this good since I was home for Christmas," Brandon said when he entered the foyer, making Eden's heart pitter-patter like the tiny feet of their future toddlers.

"I've never smelled anything this good," Jude claimed, followed by Claire's agreement and some good-natured grumbling as Brandon herded them to the bathroom to wash their hands before they ate.

When they were out of earshot, Charlene nodded sagely. "Told…you. Bread…is…a…turn-on."

"Charlene." Eden feigned shock.

"Works…on…Barney." The women laughed together, and Eden was grateful her friend was having such a good day.

As the others returned to the dining room, she stole glances at Brandon.

"Can we cut the bread now?" Jude asked, staring hungrily at the challah.

"Let's take a moment to thank the baker and our host—" Brandon began, instantly interrupted by two overly hearty *thank yous* followed by the chant, "Slice the bread! Slice the bread! Slice the bread!"

Slapping his palm against his forehead, Brandon pleaded, "People! Manners."

Obviously delighted by the chaos, Charlene thumped her hand on the arm of her chair in rhythm with the chant.

Brandon shrugged his surrender. "Fine. You're as bad as my siblings and I when we were younger."

Eden felt happy all the way down to her toes. "Why don't you do the honors," she told Brandon, smiling as he picked up the bread knife to exaggerated whoops and cheers. This was so stinkin' fun. She definitely wanted two to four kids.

When the doorbell sounded, she regretted the interruption, but chirped, "Be right back. Carry on." Hurrying, hoping to get back to the dining room as soon as possible, she yanked open the front door.

Gideon—and guest—stood on the threshold. In a complete change from this morning, he looked utterly composed, his dark hair controlled to within an inch of its life. Dark jeans and a fisherman's sweater appeared freshly laundered. The jeans may have been ironed. Weekend Gideon—casual yet impeccable. Her hand itched to reach out and mess up his hair.

He was doing his Mr. Freeze impression again, which must mean they were back to square one.

On the opposite end of the friendliness spectrum, the woman standing beside Gideon smiled generously. "I'm Layla," she said, holding out her hand when he failed to speak.

"Eden." Introducing herself, Eden accepted the handshake, noting immediately that Layla had skin as smooth as a silk sheet.

Gideon's companion was lovely. Actually, that was an understatement. Layla was hotter than a summer in Fort Worth. In addition to elbow-length dark blond waves that had been foilayaged by an expert, she had eyes the color of morning glories, a nose any plastic surgeon would have been proud to claim and a size-six figure that lent itself beautifully to a cropped sweater and flowery skirt that hugged her hips before turning into one of those flowy creations that made one think of summer breezes and fields of daisies.

Eden looked at Gideon, who was staring at her stonily, his lips in a firm line. Hard to imagine those same lips spontaneously kissing her the other night. The instant she thought of that, Eden felt heat crawl up her neck to her face.

Glancing between them with an odd look, Layla explained, "We're here to see Charlene."

"Of course." Awkwardly she stepped back. "Come in. I'll tell her you're here. Was she expecting you?"

"We have a standing appointment," Layla said as she entered the foyer, followed by Gideon.

"Barney didn't mention anything. He must have forgotten."

"I should have called to remind him."

Sounds of laughter and chatter reminded Eden of the happy scene she'd left. "Um… We're all in the dining room."

The slowest brow in the West arched. "Charlene has company," Eden told him, feeling a flicker of petty rebellion. "She's having fun." *Just like you could have if you weren't so stubborn.* Eden barely stopped herself from sticking out her tongue.

"That's wonderful." Layla's smile could have softened a boulder. "She's certainly made good progress lately. I'm glad she feels ready to socialize." Warmth poured from the woman's expression like honey from a jar. She looked so relaxed, so comfortable. "Come on." When she looped her arm through Gideon's, Eden felt her eyes widen. There couldn't be something more than a professional relationship between the two of them. Could there? They were completely different. And Gideon had made it clear he didn't want human companionship.

No, sweetie, he made it clear he didn't want yours.

"Well, we're in the dining room," she said again, shutting the front door. She had an uncomfortable feeling she couldn't name.

"Something smells wonderful, by the way," Layla complimented as they headed toward the sound of laughter.

"Challah bread," Eden said. "I made it." She didn't know why she felt it necessary to add that, but Layla perked right up.

"I love to bake bread! It's so relaxing, isn't it? I've never tried challah. Mostly I'm playing with sourdoughs right now."

Of course you are. The woman had skin so smooth a ladybug would skid across it and an affinity for baking sourdough bread. As she walked behind them, Eden frowned at the arm Layla had looped through Gideon's. Did Layla know why Gideon smashed glasses? Did she know he ate alone most of the time? If so, where was she? Why didn't she spend more time with him?

Her misgivings rose as they entered the dining room,

Charlene was glowing. Brandon had pushed her wheelchair to the head of the table, the very spot from which Charlene had always presided over Friday night Shabbat meals, her dove-gray curls covered by a lace shawl that had belonged to her grandmother, eyes closed, skin absorbing the light of the tall candles over which she prayed.

Swaying softly, Charlene would offer thanks for the week just passed, hopes for the week ahead, then pray for the people around the table and in their community and for the world at large. Always, her words and tone had been relaxed and friendly, as though the business of faith was a simple matter. Maybe faith in the world came from trusting in love? Eden had lost her trust in love before coming to Holliday. As if magnetized, her gaze locked with Gideon's, who was standing beside her now. Suddenly she knew he, too, was a casualty of love. That broken glass had to have something to do with a romance. His wariness, his retreating… A relationship had broken his faith, like it had broken hers. She was sure of it.

He swallowed as he stared back at her, the strong muscles in his neck moving. It was hard to tell if he was uncomfortable with her studying him so blatantly, but he didn't look away. If only he could have experienced the feeling at the table on those much-missed Shabbat eves…the peace, the sense that no one was alone, the momentary perfection….

She felt it now, and the desire to share it with him was so powerful it took her breath away.

"I once ate an entire pie my mother baked for Thanksgiving." Brandon's jovial voice broke the cocoon that had briefly enclosed her and Gideon. Arching a brow, he looked toward the table where Brandon sat with Charlene and the kids, feasting on bread and cheese.

"She made me make a new one," Brandon continued. "That's how I realized I enjoyed baking," he said.

"Dude, my mother would have killed me in my sleep," Jude said around a mouthful of challah and cheddar.

"No one in my family bakes," Claire complained. "It's white and sliced or it's not bread."

"That's…terrible," Charlene responded, thumping her hand on the arm of her wheelchair. "You'll… come…here. Next… Sunday. You'll…bake…cake."

"Really?" Claire tried and failed to be play it cool. "Yeah, I'd do that."

Layla approached Charlene. "It's wonderful to see you looking so well," she enthused, bending down for a hug.

Brandon pushed back his own chair and rose. "So sorry. I didn't hear you."

"No worries at all," Layla reassured. "I enjoyed listening to your story. I ate a whole batch of my mother's jam cookies once."

Brandon whistled. "Did you have to remake them?"

"No. I was so sick my mother figured that was punishment enough." They laughed. Like old friends. "I'm Layla. I'm this lovely lady's speech therapist."

"Brandon." Smiling appreciatively, he shook Layla's petal-smooth hand.

Eden glanced again at Gideon, her tongue heavy as a brick. He was watching the scene in the dining room now, and she felt awful for him. If Layla was, in fact, his partner, she had an odd way of showing it, spewing sparkly fairy dust all over Brandon... who appeared to be shooting some sparks of his own in Layla's direction.

Shoulder to shoulder, she and Gideon watched what seemed to be inevitable: two beautiful Disney-like people discovering each other. Bright, happy, full of joy, not a hint of darkness inside. Without warning, she felt Gideon's hand slip around hers. She startled, felt his fingers stiffen then squeeze hers, as if he'd suddenly realized what he'd done and decided it was the right thing. His palm was smooth and warm, the fingers elegant and strong.

Brandon seemed to realize there was someone else who hadn't been in the room previously and did the courteous thing, releasing Layla and walking over to her and Gideon.

"Hey. I'm Brandon," he introduced himself to Gideon, holding out his hand.

At that point, Eden began to pull her hand away, but Gideon stopped her. He nodded. Once. "We met."

"Did we?" Brandon tilted his head. "Sorry. I'm usually good with faces."

"There was a lot going on. It was Friday night. Right here."

"Friday night." His brow furrowed, then cleared, and he snapped his fingers. "You brought the wine. And there was that radical electric wine opener." He nodded broadly. "I've got it now. Good to see you, man."

Gideon paused before responding, "You, too."

"Hey." Brandon looked back at Layla, including her, too. "Do you want some bread? It's incredible."

He cocked a finger at Eden. "Don't worry. We'll save some for the baker." Charming as ever, he grinned, and she waited for the giddy anticipation to fizz in her veins. All she felt was her palm getting sweaty in Gideon's. She could feel his irritation with the other man. Never mind that Brandon and Layla might be getting flirty, Gideon was a serious man; his takeaway from Friday night would not be the radical electric wine opener.

"I'd love to try a slice." Layla grinned at Eden and Brandon. "My friend Roz ordered a sixty-year-old sourdough starter from a bakery in Russia and shared it with me. I made a rye bread. Just the thought of eating something with the same ingredient that someone ate sixty years ago is thrilling, isn't it? I'm only a weekend baker, but the rye did taste pretty fantastic."

Of course.

Brandon looked enthralled. And why not? He was a history teacher. Sixty-year-old Russian sourdough starter (whatever that was) trumped her challah. Still, it was just bread. The woman hadn't dug up a Faberge egg in her backyard.

A heavy torpor locked Eden in place as Brandon sliced a piece of challah and offered it to Layla, upon which they took a deeper dive into the marvels of leavening agents.

The weirdness of this moment pressed down on her. She was watching the Scotsman of her dreams delightedly trading baking secrets (put the salt on the opposite side of the mixing bowl from the sugar and yeast) with a beautiful woman and pretty much ignoring her—after he'd just asked her out! All the while she was holding hands with a man who only this morning had made it clear he did not want a relationship of any kind, but now refused to release her fingers. Abruptly, she felt very weary and decided she didn't want to eat the bread; she wished the loaves were still intact so she could bop Gideon and Brandon on the head with them. Men were confusing and difficult. Yanking her hand away from Gideon's, she crossed her arms.

She felt him glance at her, but declined to return the look this time. Moving to Charlene, Gideon knelt beside her wheelchair and placed a hand on her arm. "You look very well. Mind if I check your pulse before you get to work with Layla?"

Look at him. Being all kind and bedside mannerish. Mere hours ago he'd told her to buzz off. How could she have forgotten that?

"Oh, let her finish her party," Layla responded, smearing a second piece of bread with the butter that probably wouldn't alter her willowy body one bit. She twinkled again at Brandon, who glowed back. "I can wait."

I bet you can. In her mind, Eden's darling half-Scottish children now had blond hair. Worse still, she wasn't completely sure she cared. This afternoon was turning into a sticky, more confusing blob than her bread dough.

She wanted what Charlene and her Barney had: soul mates with a promise that lasted beyond even the future they could see. For months, her "forever" had had a face. Now the future loomed like an unmarked road—no cues about which way to turn, no clear destination.

After checking Charlene's pulse in spite of Layla's protest, Gideon traded a few quiet words with the older woman, then rose and turned to the teens, who were still stuffing themselves with bread and cheese. "How's your ankle, Jude? Does it still feel sprained?"

He knew Jude?

"Nope," The teen answered around a full mouth. He swallowed without chewing and said, "The way you showed me to wrap it really helped. I thought about what you said—about maybe studying first aid or something. You know, in case I want to try something like medicine when I get out of high school. Maybe. I don't know." He sounded embarrassed, as if he didn't think he should be aiming quite so high.

"You should try it," Gideon replied. "You asked good questions when you came to the office. And you were curious. That's a good quality for a medical professional to have. Call Janette to make an appointment after school one day this week. We'll talk again. I might even have some part-time work that would let you hang around, see what a day in a doctor's office is like."

He didn't have to do that, reach out to a kid who wore a tired-looking Jughead beanie and faded plaid flannel shirt everywhere he went. The entire town knew that Jude, who lived over in Wurst, had gotten into trouble after his father's layoff from a Holliday-family owned company last summer. Jude had ridden his bike to Holliday in the dead of night and vandalized the hardware store, including throwing a brick paver through the plate-glass window out front. Gideon had been in town for that.

Gideon's offer transformed the boy's face, his typically disgruntled expression clearing. Surprise and anticipation took over. "Yeah, okay," he said. "That'd be okay." He reached for the grape juice and offered to pour for the others. Layla chatted animatedly with Charlene. Only Eden and Gideon stood on the outside of the little party, looking in.

Uncrossing her arms, Eden approached him. "Excuse me. Do you have a moment?"

He looked at her quizzically. Her emotions were rising like a high tide, and she needed someplace for them to go. Stabbing her index finger toward the door, she requested, "I need to talk to you, please. Outside."

Chapter Ten

Aware that their presence would not be missed, Gideon walked with Eden to the Gleasons' front porch, curious when she faced him squarely, fists on her hips.

She'd been a thorn in his side since the day he'd met her. No, that wasn't accurate. She'd been disturbing his peace since the moment he'd first heard her on the patio of her apartment late one night, reenacting a hospital scene from *Gray's Anatomy* for her friend. Unable to sleep, which was nothing new, he'd gone outside hoping that the silence might quiet the noise in his head. No such luck. Eden had been talking in a variety of English accents and wondering aloud about various kissing styles. The urge to look over the fence between their small yards hit him with shocking strength.

Moving to a place where no one knew him had been meant to afford anonymity chased by a healthy dose of isolation. Portland and Salem were close enough to lend Holliday some sophistication. People would leave him alone if he made it clear he was there to provide for their basic medical needs and *nothing more*, right?

He'd miscalculated.

If he stopped at Thanksgiving for some takeout, Felipa, the restaurant's owner, demanded to know his favorite foods so she could make a special meal to thank him properly for referring her to a podiatrist. Her feet had never felt better.

Barney Gleason had insisted Gideon join them for their gathering on Friday night and refused to take no for an answer. Janette, his medical receptionist and scheduler, tried to send him on house calls no matter how many times he told her he wasn't offering that service.

And then there was Eden.

A solitary night at home was never solitary anymore, because he could hear her talking on her phone or watching TV (the woman loved her British shows) or moving around her bedroom.

The gray clouds had not parted today. A wintry breeze chilled the air, but Eden didn't look cold.

Quite the opposite. Her cheeks were flushed with what appeared to be anger. "I have a question," she said. "Do you mind if I ask you a question?"

Uh-oh. "Not at all."

"Good." She nodded. "What the hell was going on in there?"

In the months they had lived side by side, he had never seen her so upset. "What do you mea—"

"No," she cut him off. "You know what I mean. And if you don't know, you ought to. I have been trying for weeks to be friendly to you. I have been open, I have been ingratiating, I have been welcoming." She ticked the attempts off on her fingers. "I brought you cookies—all right, the beagle ate them—but it showed I was thinking about you. Friday you seemed to want to be friendly—you even kissed me, Gideon—but then you left me that stick-up-your-ass note, pardon my French, and this morning you go all Gothic Heathcliff." She lowered her voice, mimicking him. "'You don't know me. You don't know who I am. We're not alike.' Blah, blah, blah. *Then*, when I try to pull my hand away from yours, you hold on."

Her gaze was furious as she delivered an ultimatum. "This is your last chance, Gideon. Do you accept my friendship, or don't you? And if you do want my friendship, then you have to return it. I mean it. Otherwise, I'm done," she warned, actually shaking her finger at him. "No more openness, no more welcome, no more cookies." She made a big, final X with her hands. "Kaput. So—" her chin lifted, and he noticed for the first time there was a crescent-shaped scar on the underside "—what's it going to be?"

The breeze lifted locks of her mahogany hair, swirling it around her face. She'd made him smile a few times since they'd met, but today his lips didn't move. The pleasure he was feeling emanated from deep inside, from a place he hadn't felt in so long, he'd thought it didn't exist anymore.

"How did you get the scar beneath your chin?" She looked at him as if he was crazy, as if he hadn't heard a word she'd just said, so he added, "It seems like something a friend would know."

Clearly caught off guard by that, she blinked her thick lashes several times. Maybe he should have answered her directly: *Yes, I want to be your friend. Yes, I'll try harder not to be an ass. Thank you for a second (third?...fourth?) chance.* Probably he should say something like that. No, definitely he should. He couldn't yet.

She might never know the enormous gratitude he felt when she accepted exactly where he was in this moment.

"I was in a car accident. Most of my scars are on my torso," she said, and he got the feeling she was being careful yet matter-of-fact. "I got caught by a piece of shattered glass on my chin. It seemed like the least of the problems at the time, but it left a mark."

She shared the information in a near monotone. Same way he spoke when he was afraid he might reveal too much about the choice that had altered his life for good. He liked it when people took the hint and stopped asking him questions, yet found he wasn't quite ready to extend that same courtesy to Eden. He wanted to know more. "When was this?" he asked in the gentlest tone he could, even though "gentle" was no longer his forte.

"I never talk about this." She looked and sounded bemused as to why she was discussing it now. "I was fifteen. Almost sixteen." Taking a deep breath and sighing it out, she said, "Now you need to tell me something I don't know about you."

He had more questions for her, medical and otherwise, but accepted the boundary for the time being. The request—information about him—was harder to comply with, and he actually started to sweat. *I played lacrosse in college* wasn't enough. She'd admitted she didn't like to talk about her accident (and why was that?); if he responded to her reveal with some lame-ass excuse for sharing, she'd have every right to close off, and he didn't want that. For the first time in forever he wanted contact, and not with just anyone. With Eden. He began to perspire more.

"I was married." The words came haltingly,

but at least they came. "Once. We were…young."
There, that was enough. Please, let that be enough.

Eden studied him a long time, her lips moving
as if she was about to form a word, though she
didn't. He was perspiring so heavily, he had to
wipe his brow. A string of expletives ran through
his mind. The fact that he'd been married wasn't a
secret. That wasn't the issue. The issue was in the
details, and he couldn't share them all. Wouldn't.

"Thank you for telling me."

There wasn't much time for relief or gratitude
or awe that she'd read him well as the Gleasons'
front door opened, commanding their attention.

The teens spilled out, followed by Buchanan,
who exclaimed when he saw Eden, "Hey! There
you are. I've got to get this crew back to work,
but I was thinking about Silver Falls. Could be
raining next Sunday. Probably not the best hiking weather."

Gideon sensed a profound change in Eden.
Tension raised her shoulders nearly to her ears.
"Right," she responded, her voice tight as a piano
wire. "Could be raining."

So he'd asked her out? What was he doing now?
*Un*asking? Gideon took a step forward, unsure of
what he intended to do. His felt his muscles con-
tract as if preparing to fight.

"How about dinner at Thanksgiving this week?"
Buchanan asked, and Gideon froze where he was.

Buchanan's face was all boyish charm and aggravating confidence. Standing slightly behind her, Gideon saw Eden's shoulders relax, her neck and head straighten.

"Dinner," she repeated.

"Yeah. Tuesday?"

She nodded slowly. "Tuesday. Let me think… I believe I'm free. Okay, sure. Dinner at Thanksgiving on Tuesday." She was playing it cool. That was good, at least.

Buchanan grinned. "Great. Is six o'clock okay? I like to end my weeknights early since I get up at five to run with some kids who need the exercise."

"Wow. That's really nice."

Dipping his head with a humbleness that brought a giant pile of horsebunky to Gideon's mind, Buchanan beamed his Hollywood-worthy gaze at Eden. "Six o'clock, then. Can't wait."

"Six o'clock," Eden confirmed.

Gideon's teeth clenched so hard they hurt.

Buchanan waved a hand at her and loped down the steps toward the tools they'd left in the yard. Eden turned toward Gideon. "I guess we should get off their workplace."

"We should. Yeah."

She chewed the inside of her very full lower lip. "So listen, in the interest of friendship we should probably say, 'Hi,' when we see each other, occasionally watch Netflix or another mutually agreed-upon channel together, and we should stop criticizing my recycling habits."

Relief rushed through him, swift and surprising. *Yes, to all of it.* "Boxes," he stated firmly, so they'd have something to argue about, "should be broken down before being put in the bin. It makes more room."

"We don't need more room."

"If one of us were to buy a large item and if that large item were to come in a box, it's possible we would need the room." Her expression was totally worth it.

"Fine. I'm not compromising on the other two requirements, though. You have to greet me when you see me, and you have to watch Netflix."

"Or another mutually agreed-on channel."

She rolled her eyes. "Why do I bother?"

"I don't know." Gideon held out his hand. Eden took it, the feel of her skin as comforting as a cool room in the heat of summer. They let go at the same time—she, because Buchanan was heading to the porch again with his tools; he, because the temptation to hang on was too strong.

She hitched a thumb toward the front door. "Want to go back in, then?"

"No, I've got to go. Do me a favor and tell Layla I went back to the office. She can meet me back there."

"Oh. Sure."

He pushed a smile to his face, because that's what friends did. "Have fun. If I see you later at the house, I'll say 'Hi.'"

She grinned. "You do that, Dr. Bowen. See ya."

After she went back inside, Gideon headed down the walkway, returning Drew's wave, nodding briefly in response to Buchanan's.

It had been a long time since he'd wanted to punch another man in the nose. Buchanan wasn't right for Eden. That wasn't jealousy talking.

Maybe it was, partly. Didn't matter. The man was flimsy, superficial. He'd looked utterly terrified when Eden convulsed, and now he was asking her out? What the hell was that about? Was he going to be there for her when she needed him, or just for the fun parts?

Was it any of Gideon's concern?

Yes. As her *friend*, damn straight it was his business. She could do better than a man who looked for a photo op every time he said *gesundheit*.

His smile felt satisfyingly grim when he remembered that friends lasted longer than lovers. It was a universal law. Oddly, Gideon began to feel a little lighter as he strode down the block.

On Tuesday, the day before her first date with Brandon, Eden had an appointment with her doctor at OHSU in Portland. Her parents lived in Milwaukie, in the 1950s ranch-style home where she and Ryan grew up, just twenty minutes from the research hospital on Marquam Hill. She hadn't been to their family home in months.

The rest of the afternoon at Charlene and Barney's had gone well. Layla and Brandon had said goodbye to each other in a friendly but not overly friendly or flirtatious way, and Eden's anticipation was building again. Her brother's wedding was approaching, and her hopes were once again mounting that she might have her plus-one to dance with at the reception.

Maybe she'd misread Brandon's initial interactions with Layla. A case of her own insecurities at play?

Regardless of whether she had the date of her dreams, she was excited about Ry and Olli's nuptials and wanted it to be as special as possible. Weddings were meant to be enjoyed by families; they were the happiest of reunions. Get-togethers with the folks usually ended early, with their mother incapacitated from a combination of vodka Gibsons and Ativan, and their father jovially pretending surprise that his "beautiful wife got a little tipsy tonight."

His beautiful wife had been getting crocked every night since the accident that had changed all their lives. Eden felt in her gut it was time to demand back some of what they'd lost. All the family together, sober and celebrating and focused on Ryan and Ollison for their wedding—that's what she wanted, and it didn't seem like too much to ask.

In that spirit she was about to phone her parents to invite herself over after her doctor appointment. She could have called on Sunday evening when the idea had first occurred, but in her experience it was never a great idea to give Miri and Joseph Berman too much time to think.

She reached for the pumpkin latte she'd ordered from the Summit Café at OHSU, where she waited for her appointment to discuss the fainting spell and get cleared to drive again, and took a sip. Therapy had been a big part of her healing after the car accident. While she'd still been in the hospital, a nurse had taught her mindfulness, how to breathe and ground herself to counter the prickly hot, sick sensation that had made her want to run screaming through the halls (if she'd been able) when she'd gotten anxious, which had been pretty much all the time. Calling her parents generally required a shot of Mylanta, so she tried her "magic breaths," as the nurse had called them, now. Breathe in for four counts, hold five... Her head, neck and shoulders were stiff and tight, her eyes blurry as she stared hard at her cell phone. Exhale—one, two, three, four, five, six.

"Ready or not." She dialed the number, felt as

if the rings were reverberating in the center of her chest and didn't know whether to feel frustrated or relieved when her mother's voice mail began.

"This is Miri Berman. I am unavailable." *No kidding.* "Please leave a message after you hear the beep. Not before. I won't know what you've said if you speak before the beep. Regardless of how much time you think you need, kindly limit your message to only the information that is strictly necessary." Pause. "Thank you." Pause. "Have a good day." Beep.

"Hi, Mom, it's Eden. Wow, you changed your outgoing message. Really warmed it up. Listen, I'm at OHSU—" *Oh, damn. Mention of major medical institution guaranteed to send Miri to the couch with a gin and tonic.* "I had a minor medical issue— very minor—and was overdue for a physical anyway, so here I am." A couple of small fibs, but for the greater good. Anyway, I was wondering—" BEEP! *Dang it!* She called again. Waited through the message. Why did phoning her mother always seem as if she was interviewing for a dream job with insufficient qualifications?

"So," she continued, picking up the pace lest she get cut out off again, "I'm here in Portland, and I thought I'd swing by this afternoon if you and Daddy are free. Text me if you are." Her mother hated talking to voice mail. "Around four-okay-bye!" She heard the beep and felt like an Israelite who'd made it through the dry Red Sea a millisecond before the waters had rushed in again.

Dropping her phone in her purse, Eden exhaled. If her parents agreed to meet, she'd get a solid couple of hours to do a few chores around the house for them, thereby buttering them up before she addressed the real reason for her visit.

Jeremy was due to pick her up at six so they could ride back to Holliday together.

Not only had her boss given her the day off to go to the doctor, he'd dropped her at Oregon Health and Sciences University on his way to a meeting with his brother Adam, a lawyer near Lloyd Center, who handled all the Hollidays' business contracts, but only rarely made an appearance in the town that bore his name. Jeremy and Adam had business that would last the day.

Eden had already mapped out the route to her parents' place from OHSU's Marquam campus. It was a simple enough trip. She'd need to take the OHSU aerial tram to the south waterfront, then hop on the orange line and ride it all the way to Milwaukie. Easy-peasy. Well…until she walked the half mile from the MAX station to her parents' place, which was when *easy* would turn into *queasy*. Taking another sip of her latte, Eden gazed out the wall of windows before her to the glorious Portland skyline beyond. A long, long time ago, the Bermans had felt like a true family. They hadn't been a *Father Knows Best* episode, but what family truly was?

Miri had been a good mom in their early years, and very present in their lives, especially Ryan's. Her son's over-the-top accomplishments had seemed to comfort and delight her in a way nothing else could. She'd accompanied him to every sporting event, each debate team or robotics competition. The accident had changed things.

However acceptably dysfunctional their family had been before, after the accident they didn't seem to fit together anymore, like a puzzle whose pieces had frayed until they no longer snapped together. And in all the years since, they'd never managed to heal the wounds that had fragmented them.

Now, Ryan's wedding was a mere ten weeks away. Miri rarely socialized these days. If she and Joe did make an appearance, it was assumed they would arrive late and leave quickly, and Ry was fine with that. But weddings were family gatherings of significance. Happiness…laughter…futures filled with promise. Maybe a joyous occasion like this one would inspire a new beginning for all of them. They'd been waiting a long time for that.

Eden drank some more of her latte, grateful for its warmth. She'd had enough therapy to know that she was trying to put her family of origin back together to prove to herself that she could have a healthy family of her own. Ryan liked to rib her about wanting a "Mayberry" life. Maybe she did. (Definitely she did.) So sue her. Who fantasized about creating a family rife with friction, or celebrations that ended in utter frustration for everyone? Exactly no one, that's who. Could she be blamed for trying to create something more?

The alarm on Eden's phone tinkled with a fairy sound, alerting her that it was time to head to her doctor's office.

Rising, she dropped her coffee cup in the trash as the nauseating kind of nerves that had no redeeming value filled her stomach, churning the latte into a sour soup. Intuition told her the fainting spell wasn't indicative of anything serious, and her doctor had agreed after listening to Eden describe her symptoms over the phone. Still, with her history, no visit to the hospital on the hill was without anxiety. She'd spent a lot of time at Doernbecher, the children's hospital. Miri would buy them blueberry scones and hot cocoa before Eden's appointments with her burn specialist. She must have done the same for Ryan before his appointments with his neurosurgeon.

Distracted by her thoughts, Eden almost ran into a sign. Large, as tall as she was, positioned in the middle of the bank of elevators so it couldn't be missed, it stopped her cold. She stared at it, disbelieving.

"Are you going?" A woman with silver hair below her shoulders and big dangly earrings stood to her left.

Two elevators opened. Eden needed to get on one of them. "Excuse me?" she asked, unsure whether the woman was referring to the elevators or the sign.

"To his lecture," the lady clarified, pointing a long pink fingernail at the photo of Gideon's—her Gideon's—smiling face. In a white coat and blue dress shirt, the upper portion of his broad torso visible in a three-quarter turn, Gideon looked into the camera as if it were an old friend. "I went to a panel discussion he was on a couple years ago," the woman continued, "back when I thought I was *finito*." Using her index finger, she drew a line across her neck, then released a booming laugh.

Their conversation had just begun and already Eden had lost the thread, possibly because her focus was stolen by her landlord's portrait. The photo had to be a few years old. In addition to appearing younger, Gideon looked happier, heavier, fuller in every way.

"Finito?" she asked the woman, looking into vivid blue eyes enhanced with sparkly lavender shadow.

"The big 'C.' Stage four. Doctors wanted to shoot me up with chemicals for a few months so I could enjoy watching my hair fall out while I got my affairs in order. Seemed like a crap way to check out, if you ask me. Which nobody did." She rapped her knuckles on Gideon's image. "Except this guy. He told me I was in charge. Saved my ass. Not to mention my life." She offered another hearty belly laugh.

Eden smiled, but shook her head. "I'm not sure I understand what you mean. How did he save your life?"

"Sorry, I stopped my ADD meds. I'm a chemical-free zone. Also my blood sugar's probably low. Maybe I should have a Kind bar." She began to rummage through a large shoulder bag while she talked. "Doc Gideon's not like a lot of the other bigwigs with their protocols and statistics—and my statistics were crap, let me tell you. Doc Gideon told me, 'Sheila, you are not a number. You're a human being, and human beings are surprising creatures.' Isn't that nice? Surprising creatures. So, I decided to surprise everyone." Abandoning the search for a snack in her purse, she muttered, "Ah, I must have left it at home. Anyway, after Doc Gideon reminded me I have choices, I chose to heal my way." She raised her arms, flexing like a bodybuilder. "Sixty-seven years young, and I'm the fittest I've ever been, minus a gallbladder and a couple feet of intestine, but I hardly miss them. Also, my high kick is better than ever."

"But…um…" How to put this exactly? "Isn't his lecture about—" Eden glanced quickly at the sign "—assisted suicide?"

The title of the workshop was "Physician-Assisted Dying, Rights and Responsibilities."

"Yeah." Sheila nodded. "So what's your story? Are you interested for yourself or somebody else?"

"Neither. I'm here for a doctor's appointment. I'm not going to his lecture."

"Too bad. If you've never heard him speak, it's a treat."

Eden smiled vaguely, wondering if she knew Gideon at all. It seemed there were two Gideons. Or three. The uptight landlord, the mysterious glass-throwing stranger, the compassionate doctor with interest in end-of-life issues.

And then there was Gideon number four, the one who spontaneously kissed a friend. It was all too puzzling. Flipping her wrist, Eden checked the time. Eight minutes until her appointment.

"I've got to head to my appointment, but it was great to meet you, Sheila." She took a couple of steps toward the elevator. "Congratulations on your remarkable recovery."

"Thanks, sweetie. If you're done in time, try to come back for the doc's lecture. It's a mind blower!"

Eden nodded as she pressed the call button for

the elevator. A mind-blowing lecture. Not hard to believe. It didn't take much these days to blow her mind where Gideon was concerned.

Chapter Eleven

Approximately an hour and a half after meeting Sheila, Eden had offered up her arm for blood tests, scheduled an EEG "to err on the safe side," according to her doctor, and, most bothersome of all, had agreed not to get behind the wheel of a car until all the results had come back. "An abundance of caution," Marisa Robillard, her doctor for the past twenty years, had assured, adding, "I suspect everything will test out fine. Dr. Bowen is excellent, and he's probably correct in suggesting low blood sugar as the driving factor here. Make sure you're hydrated well, too."

Eden had tried to weasel a little info about

Gideon out of Marisa, but all the doctor would offer was that Gideon had been affiliated with OHSU for "a long time" and that she was aware he'd "developed an interest in end-of-life issues." Eden found it strange that she and Gideon had quite probably been in the same building a number of times throughout the years. Maybe they'd even seen each other or stood in line for a veggie burger without realizing it.

Stepping off the elevator on the ground level, Eden fished her phone out of her purse and listened to her voice mails. The only call she'd missed was from her father.

"Hello, buttercup!" his voice boomed, using the nickname she'd loved in her childhood. "Mom said you're on the hill. Routine visit, I hope? Listen, I'm calling from work. Mommy says you want to stop by the house this afternoon. Gee, we'd love to see you, but your mother hasn't been feeling well. Probably only a bit of a cold, but we don't want you to catch anything." He paused briefly to tell someone where to find an elbow joint for a toilet, then returned to the call. "I've got to run, buttercup. They expect me to work around here!" Another hearty burst of laughter. "Call me later. Okey dokey?"

Eden's jaw clenched. It was not okey dokey. It was inky stinky. Her mother didn't have a cold. Miri never caught a cold. "Headache," "runny nose," "stomach bug"—all code for "Took a pain pill the size of a golf ball and chased it with a gin and tonic." That was what Eden wanted to discuss tonight—the chemical and alcohol dependency that had destroyed any semblance of the family they'd once been. And her father didn't want to touch the topic with a ten-foot pole. He never did. Ryan had long ago given up hoping for change. Said he felt better that way. What was the saying— "Expectations are resentments under construction"? Eden had begun the day expecting to repair her family in time for Ryan's wedding. The disappointment was tremendous. She didn't want to resent her parents, didn't want to blame them for not being better, but it was tough.

Dropping the phone back into her purse, she walked past the sign with Gideon's picture. Without visiting her parents, she'd have quite a bit of time to kill before Jeremy would be ready to head back to Holliday.

She stopped and studied Gideon's sign. "Physician-Assisted Dying, Rights and Responsibilities." *He developed an interest in end-of-life issues.* On Sunday, she'd asked him to tell her something about himself, something she hadn't already known (which was nothing other than the obvious), and he'd said he'd been married once. She'd had to clamp her teeth onto her tongue to keep from peppering him with questions after that. It had been so obvious to her that he hadn't wanted to elaborate, at least in that moment. Weird as it sounded, she felt a little voyeuristic at this public lecture. Would he want her here? Now that they were becoming friends—they really were; he'd been pretty adorable Sunday afternoon, and that was not an adjective she'd ever imagined ascribing to Gideon—she had the feeling she should wait for him to give her any information he wanted her to have. To say he was private was the world's biggest understatement.

And yet, there were a lot of people here. A lot of people who already knew or would soon know more about him than Eden did. So, even as something inside whispered to her to wait, that he would want to tell her about himself in his own time, curiosity won. Twenty minutes later, she stood at the door to his lecture, scanning the crowd of fifty or so people who were already seated, telling herself she was merely observing. Just curious to see how many people would show up.

"Hi, honey!" Sheila appeared at Eden's elbow. "Oh, good, you brought snacks." She nodded at the packet of whole-grain pretzels and hummus Eden had picked up in the cafeteria and raised a bag, showing off her own selection of workshop treats. "I got Chicago corn. I'll share. Where should we sit?"

"I'm not staying. I'm going to sit outside and eat—"

"There! Two seats together." She grabbed

Eden's arm, singing "Excuse me" to a man on the aisle while pointing down his row. "Are those seats taken?"

"Sheila," Eden protested, "I'm not staying."

"What? Why not? Come on." Sheila tugged on Eden again, commencing to edge her way in front of the row, large purse and snack bag swinging so that everyone leaned back while turning in their seats to allow the flamboyant woman to pass.

"Sheila," Eden hissed. "I'm not staying. It was nice to meet you—"

"Could you choose a seat?" complained the woman in front of whom Eden had stalled. "I can't see the front of the room."

"Of course. I'm just going to back up—"

"Come on!" Sheila waved at her energetically. "The doc's here. They're going to start."

Eden looked around, spotting Gideon at the door through which she, too, had entered and beginning to walk up the aisle. How was she going to get out of here? The far end of the row was flanked by a wall.

The woman behind her spoke again. "I don't see a stop sign. Do you see a stop sign?"

Eden dived toward the seat Sheila was saving for her.

"Hey!" protested a different woman whose legs she'd practically hugged on her way to the seat.

"Sorry, sorry!" Eden apologized.

"This should be fascinating," Sheila told Eden in a stage whisper. "See those people walking with the doc? He helped their loved ones pass on. They come to all these shindigs with him."

Quickly, Eden pretended to search for something in her purse, her head down, hair covering her face. When she sensed they'd passed her row, she looked up, watching as they made their way along with two other people to the podium. When they reached the slightly raised stage, Gideon traded a few words with his companions before taking his place behind the microphone as they settled onto folding chairs lined up in a row behind him. He tapped a thin sheaf of papers on the stand, aligning them neatly (so Gideon), then straightened his tie and looked out at his audience.

"Good afternoon. I seem to be running on time, quite a feat for a doctor. I'd like to preserve my winning streak, so let's get started." Laughter around the room. "I'm Gideon Bowen. I'm a doctor of internal medicine, and this talk is titled 'Physician-Assisted Dying, Rights and Responsibilities.' I want to make sure you all know where you are, because I understand there's a class called Diabetic Desserts in the same time slot, and they're giving out samples." More laughter. "Last chance to leave before we start the recording." He paused a beat. "No? All right. You can't say I didn't offer."

Eden glanced around. People were shifting on

their chairs, getting more comfortable, relaxing. *Wowzer.* Gideon, the man who could make a jelly doughnut feel guilty for not being more serious, was making friends with the audience through humor and charm.

Most of Gideon's audience appeared to be in their fifties and up with a few younger people here and there. Eden didn't spend much time studying the people around her, though; she was far more interested in the man at the front of the room.

"Like many of you, I never gave much thought to end-of-life issues," he began. "I went to medical school. My ambition was—and still is—to heal. I wasn't prepared for the curveballs life threw." Gideon took a moment before continuing. "My wife had a neurological disease. It was progressive and incurable."

Eden heard her own intake of breath. He was a widower. She'd automatically assumed his was a tale of divorce, like hers. But no, Gideon, who was protective and a natural caretaker—he really was—had been in love with someone whose death had been a foregone conclusion, not something in the distant future.

"When Julianne's body began to fail her, my response was to rely on medicine to address her needs. If there was a clinical trial available, we signed up. When there were no more avenues left to us—no cures, no experimental treatments we hadn't already tried, no new miracles of science—I trusted medicine to ease her pain." He paused, brows pulled so low it almost looked as if they were trying to shade his eyes from the glare of the past. "How should we measure pain? How do you or I gauge the amount of suffering someone else should endure?"

Eden glanced around to see if anyone else was tearing up. Sheila had opened a granola bar and was chewing. Was it awful that Eden wasn't sure she wanted to hear any more?

The drink Gideon had thrown against the wall and every moment he had seemed distant, cold or preoccupied took on an entirely new meaning. Her throat felt dry and prickly when she swallowed.

"Julianne decided that if she couldn't control how she was living…" Gideon's jaw tightened; she could see it. He glanced down at the papers on the podium even though he seemed to be speaking extemporaneously. "…she wanted some control over when and how she died. That choice can be uncomfortable, even unacceptable to a patient's loved ones. I hope that demystifying the process may be able to narrow the gap between what our dying loved ones want and what we think we can tolerate. In that spirit, I'd like to give you a practical overview of what happens when someone choose physician-assisted dying as an option when nearing the end of their lives." He glanced back at

Layla and the other people with him at the front of the room. "I have a few good friends here who will walk us through the journey from a terminal diagnosis to an end-of-life decision and how you might support someone, even if you disagree with their plan."

Eden could not take her eyes off Gideon as he introduced his guests, his voice and entire demeanor deeply respectful. As each person stepped to the podium and began to share heartbreaking stories of loss, confusion and ultimately selflessness, Gideon seemed to withdraw, his mind miles away.

Thinking of his wife? Immediately, Eden got the image of a beautiful blonde, fit and lovely until the neurological disease robbed her of abilities big and small. Had they been happy? Eden wondered, deciding that of course they had been very happy, supported by family and friends. She'd bet anything they'd had a picture-book wedding, lots of toasts, with Gideon taking the mic at the reception to thank everyone for coming and to publicly express his gratitude that the most perfect woman in the world had agreed to marry a cranky, workaholic doctor. Except maybe he hadn't been cranky and a workaholic back then. Maybe that hadn't happened until his wife had become ill, and he'd realized that despite his medical training and connections he was powerless to save her.

Eden didn't realize she was crying until she felt a tear drop onto her clasped hands. Sniffling far less elegantly than she wished, she scrounged in her purse for a stray tissue, abandoning the search when one appeared in front of her face.

"It's okay, sweetie," Sheila assured in her non-stage whisper, "it gets to everyone their first time around. Would you like a caramel?"

Eden declined the candy, but accepted the tissue, blowing her nose as quietly as possible. She and Sheila were seated a good three-quarters of the way back in a decently packed room, and so far Gideon hadn't glanced her way. Keeping her head down, she stayed seated throughout the question-and-answer period. She rose immediately when the audience began to disperse. Though a small crowd surrounded Gideon and the other speakers, most people made their way to the doors in the back of the room.

Grabbing her chance to escape undetected, Eden clutched her purse and said goodbye to Sheila.

"You're not staying to ask questions? They might go out for coffee and invite a few of us along."

"No, I have to go." And, could use a martini right about now, not another coffee. After Sheila's hug, Eden sneaked out. She headed straight for the aerial tram, not pausing until she was sure there was adequate distance between her and Gideon. Then she phoned Jeremy to tell him there'd been a change of plans and that he could pick her up at The Old Spaghetti Factory on the south waterfront. In the bar.

The next night, Eden walked up Liberty Street trying to push thoughts of Gideon out of her head. She had a date with Brandon, the beginning she'd been hoping for, and that deserved her focus.

She had to have been wrong about Brandon and Layla flirting. She'd probably been wrong about Layla and Gideon being together, too. They hadn't seemed romantic at all. As she'd tearfully told the story of her husband, a twenty-nine-year-old school counselor with a glioblastoma multiforme, Gideon had listened respectfully, but with no more compassion than he'd shown the others. At least Eden now had a better understanding of the pain that drove him. Of course he was haunted by the memory of his late wife. He hadn't given any details, but he didn't have to. Knowing Gideon better now, Eden could easily imagine that he'd loved his wife as seriously as he did everything else.

Breathing deeply, Eden let the crisp night air relax her. Three weeks into November, the town clothed itself in all the trappings of the holiday season. Hand-painted messages of fellowship and gratitude graced every store window, heralding

Thanksgiving, which was only a week away now. With Hanukkah beginning a mere three days later, the community menorah was already being constructed in Liberty Park, affectionately known as the Town Circle, and soon strings of blue and silver lights in the shape of dreidels would hang from streetlamp to streetlamp.

In Holliday, as with all religious and cultural celebrations, Hanukkah received a community-wide embrace. Typically, Barney and Charlene hosted the annual latke contest in the kitchen of Holliday Community Church on the second night of candle lighting. Eden had never entered, of course, not with her terrible cooking and absolute lack of latke experience. Ariel Keiler won every year with her Secret-Ingredient Potato Latkes (the secret being the small addition of boiled and mashed parsnip added to the grated potato along with a pinch of nutmeg). After Ariel's thirteenth win in a row, Charlene had plied the titleholder with dry Rob Roys until she'd parted with the recipe. As the Gleasons were taking a break from their hosting duties this year, Ariel had agreed to give her food processor a rest and assume the role of emcee.

At Sweet Holly's, Holly Holliday, Jeremy's first cousin (and, yes, everyone felt sorry she'd been saddled with that name), would be turning out *sufganiyot*, a.k.a. jelly doughnuts, by the dozen for the community party the first night.

Eden had always loved Hanukkah, the joy of it and the fun. Ryan and Olli held a holiday open house each year—mistletoe for Olli, menorahs for Ryan. Eden had been joining them for years, but when she was married she'd imagined her own house filled with candlelight and good smells. She'd have at least four menorahs—one for each member of the family—and she'd learn the prayers and the songs (maybe she'd play the ukulele!) and watch her own kids' faces shine with wonder.

The image filled her with anticipation as she walked along the sidewalk on her way to meet Brandon. Night had already fallen, yet Liberty Street was alight as always with sparkles and twinkles. When she reached Thanksgiving restaurant, Eden felt her heart speed up. Before she opened the door, she took a deep breath to steady her nerves. No point in telling herself this was "just a first date," not when she knew it could change her entire life. Brandon's entire life, too, and the lives of their future children. Just a date? Nah. Tonight could be the beginning of her real life.

Taking one last deep inhalation, she reached for the door handle. *This is it. Day One of her long-awaited forever.*

Okay, it was just a first date.

Thirty minutes after walking in the door of Thanksgiving and requesting a table for two,

Eden sat at a booth with two menus, two glasses of water, two place settings and one her. No Brandon.

Valentina, who knew she was waiting for her date to arrive, kept darting worried glances her way. Valentina's mother, Felipa, had emerged from the kitchen three times already with a plate of complimentary appetizers—mini empanadas in the shape of wedding bells. Not too subtle, but very sweet. She had to keep taking them back to the kitchen to rewarm. On the most recent trip, Eden had heard Felipa tell her daughter, *"No riegues una planta muerta."*

Eden remembered just enough third-year Spanish to translate: *don't water a dead plant*.

Holy heaven, this couldn't be happening. Brandon wouldn't stand her up. Would he?

Eden felt her mood plummet with each pointless peek at her phone to see if he'd texted. She could call him...just to make sure he was okay. Or to make sure he remembered their date was tonight; he had a very busy schedule—all that service work. He could have legitimately gotten confused. Her right index finger moved to the screen until her brain intervened. *Humiliating. You are not going to do that.*

Or, she could phone Nikki, her happily engaged-to-be-married best friend, and sob out her fear that she was never going to have a soul mate or be a wife and mother, ever ever ever.

Um, no. Refer to "humiliating," above.

Anyway, the traditional twenty-minute grace period had elapsed ten minutes ago, and she knew what Nikki, who could be tough as nails in situations like this, would tell her: "Take the empanadas and *go*."

Tears prickled Eden's nose and began to well in her eyes. Putting her head down, she reached for her purse, freezing as she heard the door to the restaurant open. A moment later, Valentina said brightly, "Good evening! So nice to see you!" and Eden's heart began to skitter again, only to thud to the pit of her stomach when the young woman followed up with, "Are you getting something to go?"

Okay, that's it. I am not going to be this person. I have been fine alone. I will continue to be fine alone. She began to scoot to the edge of the booth, but when the new arrival came into view, led by Valentina, Eden felt her throat clog with tears.

Gideon caught her eye and raised two fingers to his forehead in greeting. The first thing she thought of was the moment he'd taken her hand at the Gleasons,' and the desire to run to him and pour out her sorrow and frustration nearly overwhelmed her. Unfortunately, risking more rejection tonight wasn't an option. Picking up the menu, she looked down, pretending to study it, even though unshed tears blurred the page.

This was awful. How was she going to leave

without making it hideously obvious she'd been stood up by the man everyone knew she was nuts about?

She tried to think through the static buzzing in her brain. This was the first time she'd seen Gideon since his workshop at OHSU. He'd gotten home very late that night, leaving again early this morning, and while her curiosity about him and his past was now more intense than ever, she was also more reticent about poking her nose where he didn't want it.

How was she supposed to play this moment? Be authentic? Stand up, laugh it off, walk out with her head held high? Or admit that at thirty-six her love life was defined primarily by the men who *weren't* interested?

Her phone rang. Pulling it from her purse, she checked the display, felt her heart go into atrial fibrillation and answered, "Hi."

"I'm so sorry." Brandon's voice was as warm and comforting...*intended* to be comforting...as ever. "Eden, I owe you more than an apology, but there's an emergency on the island, and I've got to go home."

"Oh. I'm sorry." An emergency. On the island where he'd lived most of his life. That could be honest. And serious. It was wrong to feel relief. But she did, and so she leaned into concern to balance it out. "Someone in your family? Is there anything I can do?"

There was a brief pause. "Wow, that's very generous of you after I stood you up."

"No, not at all. You couldn't help it." She hoped he couldn't help it. The glass face of her phone felt cool against her hot cheek. "And you phoned, you know, so…thank you."

"Look, I've got to go. I need to put in for a sub for my classes and get on the road. I'll call you when I get back."

Which would be…? "Sure. Let me know if you think of any way I can help."

Another pause. "You really are a sweetheart."

She smiled into the phone. What she truly wanted to do was ask what the emergency was, how long he'd be gone, whether he'd like to Face-Time while he was away. "Be safe," was all she said, though, exhibiting admirable restraint and maturity, if she did say so.

Brandon rang off, and Eden looked up to see Valentina and Felipa staring at her, their expressions less than genial. Gideon waited for his take-out. The restaurant was quiet tonight. Obviously they'd all heard her conversation. Ridiculous small town. "My date had a family emergency," she announced firmly, adding in the face of the restaurant owners' disbelieving frowns, "He's leaving for Washington in a few minutes." Brandon hadn't actually said the emergency involved his family. But it probably did.

Felipa shrugged and walked back to the kitchen.

Gideon stood silently, stoic and thoughtful, his expression almost kind, which at the moment felt like pity, and she couldn't take that right now. Rising, she donned her coat, slung her purse over her shoulder and said, "Well, I'm going to head out." She smiled serenely (she hoped) at Gideon. "Enjoy your dinner."

Walking past, she tried to look straight ahead. *Dignity*—that was her middle name tonight.

"Wait!" Felipa called, bustling out of the kitchen and hurrying to Eden before she could leave. *"Aqui, tomo esta,"* she said, concern creasing her face as she pushed a white to-go box into Eden's hands. "Take this, *querida*. The empanadas. And remember—always have a date in a restaurant you like, so if the date ends *very bad*, you will still have a good meal."

Chapter Twelve

He was not trying to take care of Eden.

Or protect her. Or save her. Or change her. He simply felt bad she'd been stood up.

Vacillating outside his neighbor's front door, Gideon checked his watch, attempting to convince himself it was okay to knock. Ten o'clock on Tuesday night, her bedroom light was still on; he could tell by the glow spilling from her patio onto his. (He wasn't stalking.)

Looking at the bag in his hand, Gideon sighed. Tonight had to have hurt, given Eden's obvious infatuation with the football coach. Or history teacher. Or youth leader. Whatever Buchanan was.

He'd come into the office during the flu shot clinic in October, but hadn't wanted an exam of any kind. Although Gideon hadn't interacted with him, he'd heard Buchanan charming his nurse—same voice the man had used with Layla. And Eden.

She was going to get hurt. That ridiculous excuse about standing her up, because he'd had an emergency? Total crock, yet Gideon was afraid Eden might fall for it. Emergencies happened, sure. *(That's what cell phones are for, asshat.)* Buchanan should have texted her right away. While sitting in the restaurant, Eden's brave expression had covered confusion and insecurity. She shouldn't be with someone who made her feel insecure.

Gideon raised his hand to knock on her door, then hesitated. Again, not stalking, not trying to take care of her, not attempting to change anyone. He had, however, wondered—*once*; he'd wondered about it once—what life would be like with Eden. He saw them somewhere sunny. A beach. Tahiti, maybe. He was carrying her, pretending he was going to toss her in the ocean. She was laughing, her arms around his neck, and for a moment the toxic gray fog in his chest dissipated, leaving sunshine.

You're getting involved. This is a bad idea. With his fingers clenched into fists, he gave three hard, fast knocks before he had a chance to stop himself.

Jackass. Him this time, not Buchanan. And, just in case he wasn't enough of a schmuck, he knocked again a little louder so he couldn't tell himself she hadn't heard him. You know what he'd do? He'd give her thirty seconds. If she didn't open the door by then, he'd go home and act like tonight never happened. *One...two...three...four...* "Hi."

Eden glared at him. "It's ten."

He made a show of checking his watch. "It is." She was wearing fuzzy dark blue pajama bottoms and a matching top that read, *Imagine if your cell phone was at 10 percent, but lasted eight days. Now you understand Hanukkah.* "Is it Hanukkah already?" he asked.

"I'm getting a head start. Do you want a jelly doughnut?"

Her tone was still less than warm, but she hadn't told him to get lost. "Do you have any?"

"I do."

"Actually, I brought ice cream." He raised the bag in his hand.

After looking from his face to the bag and back up to his face, she said, "Fine," turned and walked into the apartment, leaving him on the threshold. Eden's broad smile was usually as constant a part of her as her nose, which made her grim expression tonight all the more disconcerting.

Gideon walked in, closing the door behind him. He waited alone in the living room for a few seconds until Eden returned with one bowl and two spoons.

Moving to her sofa, which was a deep blue velvety thing as dramatic as she usually was, she sat down, crossed her legs beneath her and gestured at the bag. "What'd you bring?"

Gideon opened the bag and withdrew two pints. "Dark Chocolate Gingerbread and Brandied Eggnog. I went with a winter theme." He felt awkward about his choices, having no idea what she liked. Also, it had been years since he'd spontaneously shown up at a woman's apartment at night. Maybe he'd never done it.

Without a word, she filled the single bowl with half gingerbread ice cream, half eggnog and handed it to him along with a spoon.

"Aren't you going to have any?" he asked.

She looked at him as if he was clueless. "I'm having the rest." Grabbing a magazine, she set it on the sofa cushion, placed both chilly pints on top and started eating.

He watched her as she took her time to spoon ice cream from the cartons into her mouth, saying nothing, perfectly comfortable, it seemed, with his presence and silence. He, on the other hand, felt uncomfortable as hell.

Eden's hair was long and damp and curling, her skin free from makeup and adorably freckled. Yeah, *adorably*. He never thought words like that.

The bottoms of her socks had writing on them; she liked clothing with a message, apparently. He tried to read her soles while she tasted each ice cream flavor in turn, then tried them both at the same time.

Walk your own path. That was the message. She sure did that. She was unique—bold, sassy as hell, empathetic (kept attempting to be friends with a closed-off, isolationist grouch who'd behaved like an ass ever since she'd met him), funny and beautiful.

"Men suck." The comment popped out of her suddenly. She continued to eat her ice cream, not looking at him, just shaking her head.

He'd always wondered why there weren't more men around her place. "Yeah. There are times that we definitely do suck," he agreed, adding a mental apology to his brethren. "You like that one guy, though. The teacher."

Her eyes did dart to him at that point. She looked wary.

Gideon began eating. "Had an emergency come up tonight?"

She slammed the carton of Brandied Eggnog on the coffee table. "Yes, it *was* an emergency. A real emergency. Why does everyone assume someone is faking when they say they have an emergency?"

"I didn't say that." *Out loud.* "Did someone else suggest that?"

Plunging her spoon into the gingerbread ice cream, she answered around a mouthful. "My friend Nikki. I don't think she likes Brandon. She doesn't trust him for some reason, and, you know, I think she's projecting, because something is going on in her relationship with her fiancé." She wagged the spoon at him. "You want to talk denial? That relationship is just not right, but I don't say anything, because she's so happy about getting married. Anyway, maybe *I'm* projecting onto her, because of my stinky marriage. I was married before. Did I tell you that?"

"No."

"Well, I was. Married my high school 'sweetheart.'" She made air quotes. "He wasn't a sweetheart. He sucked. Total narcissist. I've been forgiving him for years when I should have told myself, 'Eden, face it—you married a putz. And you stayed with a putz, because you didn't have confidence in yourself.'"

"Why didn't you have confidence in yourself?"

That question elicited a long pause and required several spoonfuls of ice cream before she answered. "I suppose I never had an overabundance. My brother, Ryan, was the family success story. I was pretty average."

"I find that hard to believe."

She gave him a sad kind of smile. "I didn't mind being average. Average is highly underrated." Sticking her spoon in the Dark Chocolate Gingerbread, she leaned back and stretched her arms. Because he was male, he noticed the way the words on her pajama top stretched over her breasts.

And noticed she wasn't wearing a bra.

And noticed all the places his body was tight with desire.

"So…" His voice was froggy. He coughed to clear it. "So if being average was okay with you, what hurt your self-esteem?"

The curtain of dark, curling hair fell over her shoulder as she tilted her head to consider the question. "Being less than average." Setting both cartons of ice cream and their magazine placement on the coffee table, she stretched out her legs.

Her feet rested just shy of his thigh. A small shift to the left, and he'd be able to take them onto his lap and massage her soles while she talked, but he didn't, sensing she'd stop talking altogether… which in a way would have been fine with him. Every last drop of testosterone demanded they stop talking and start touching. He couldn't allow it. He wouldn't be good for Eden—not that way. This was not a woman who wanted a sexual relationship and nothing else. He was no longer a man who could accept anything more.

"Less than average, huh?" He shook his head. "Not buying it."

"Car accident at the age of fifteen. Third-degree

burns and contusions over thirty percent of my torso. Splenectomy required, and contracture scarring only partially alleviated and sometimes exacerbated by multiple surgeries."

"Where's the scarring?"

She didn't flinch. "On my stomach and hips mostly. Some on the tops of my thighs."

He nodded. Eden was beautiful—giant eyes, lips that were soft and curved and natural, thick hair that curled when she allowed it, and a sprinkle of freckles across creamy skin. Whatever issues she had with her body when her clothes were off, the shape of it could bring a man to his knees. At fifteen, she'd been in the early days of discovering her power as a sensuous, sexual woman. Disfigurement had to have interrupted that discovery.

"Did you know your high school sweetheart before the accident?"

"Yep." She crossed her arms, lowered her chin and arched a brow. "Before you assume he wanted to be with me because of my sparkling personality and our endless love, you should know that he got a lot of respect for staying with the burned girl. He wrote an essay about unconditional love that was published as an op-ed by the *Oregonian*. It was really good. Got picked up by 'World News Tonight.' Three years later, he contacted the producer of our segment to tell them he was going to propose, and they televised that. He wasn't good at sports and didn't have many hobbies, so he'd never felt very special in high school."

The only words that ran through Gideon's mind began with *ass*—except for the ones that started with an *F* and ended in *bastard*.

"How long did you stay with him?" Gideon asked.

She grunted with a puff of laughter that was anything but humorous. "Until he left me."

Gideon felt his anger growing. "What?"

"Yes. He wasn't even original. He left me for Yogi Jenni, my Yoga for Fertility instructor. She was really flexible." Eden took another huge bite of ice cream then, stuck the spoon in the carton of Brandied Eggnog and pushed it away. "I think I'm drunk."

"Sugar drunk, maybe."

When she picked at her thumbnail, he noticed she'd removed the long bright red nails that had seemed to be her signature. Now her fingernails were short, blunt and bare. Hesitantly, she raised her gaze to his. "Do you think Brandon's emergency was just an excuse?"

Damn it. "No." She made a face at him. He doubled down. "What guy in his right mind would duck out on the chance to date the most interesting woman in Holliday?"

For a moment she merely stared. Then without warning, Eden tucked her legs beneath her, rose to

her knees and kissed him. And not just "kissed"—
she was *kissing* him. Present tense. Continuously.

Gideon told himself…yelled it in his head,
actually…to push her away for both their sakes.
Instead of taking her firmly by the shoulders, however, holding her away from him and explaining
exactly why the two of them would never work out,
he put his hands on her back, pulling her closer so
he could feel her against him, one hand moving to
the back of her head, his fingers threading through
the thick strands, and he was undeniably kissing
her back. As if his life depended on it.

If there was a drink called Sex on the Beach to
commemorate an enjoyable but sandy interlude,
then there should also be a drink called Sex on the
Couch, Eden decided as she lay in her bedroom,
smiling at the ceiling. Granted, she hadn't had sex
on a beach (yet), but she didn't think it could be
any hotter than what had happened on her couch
with Gideon last night, and it was a lot less sandy.
In fact, there should be a drink called Sex in Bed
at 2:00 a.m., which had also been quite amazing.
Who'd have guessed?

Turning her head, she tried to make his features
out in the dark. The digital clock on her nightstand read "3:45." He was sleeping in—happily,
she hoped. She was happy. Happier than she could
have imagined.

If anyone had told her last month…heck, last week…that she and The Lord of the Duplex would be together romantically, she'd have choked on laughter. Yet here they were. He could have gone back to his place after the couch affair, but he hadn't. Instead, he'd pulled her close, running a finger along the collar of the T-shirt she'd put on.

"Sure you don't want to take this off?" he'd murmured.

With a guilty flush he hadn't seen, because she hadn't allowed him to turn on the lights, she'd answered, "Not yet."

He'd said, "Okay," then kissed her neck, her collarbone, her breasts and, finally, beneath the T-shirt and still in the dark, her stomach.

He'd felt her scars and hadn't flinched. Quite the contrary; he'd touched her tenderly—never hesitantly—giving her stomach as much attention as the rest of her. She'd felt breathless and excited and beautiful.

They'd fallen asleep with his arm across her stomach. She hadn't expected to make love with Gideon (to launch herself at him, let's be honest), but in the moment, she'd sensed she was coming to the end of something—her fantasies about Brandon—and there was Gideon, solid and reliable and *present*. And, looking at her as if he saw her exactly as she was and liked it. In that moment, all their sparring, all the connection she'd felt—it had all walloped her in the solar plexus, so she'd kissed him, and he'd kind of taken over from there.

In the wee hours of the morning, she'd lain awake as he'd begun to breathe deeply in sleep (no snoring yet; score another point for the big guy), and she'd loved the feel of his body—the strong muscles, the rough hair over the smooth skin on his arm. It had filled her with the most stirring sense of excitement and utter comfort.

Gideon was still a mystery, too much of a mystery. He hadn't yet disclosed nearly enough about himself, but she would give him some time.

His arm was still across her stomach. Gingerly, she lifted it, easing herself away and slipping out of bed. So very much had changed in less than twenty-four hours, and she needed a little space to process it. Grabbing her robe (flannel, seriously needed something sexier), she threw it around her and left the room as quietly as she could.

Malfoy had retired to the living room after several long, protesting yowls regarding the sleeping arrangements. Turning on a lamp, she noted immediately that he, too, had wound up having a pretty good night. She and Gideon had forgotten the ice cream cartons on the coffee table. Brandied Eggnog was on the floor, licked clean. Dark Chocolate Gingerbread was upended on the table, its contents melted and sticky as Malfoy curled in a ball on the back of the sofa, intoxicated by a night of hard eating.

Going to the kitchen for cleaning supplies, she considered the contents of her pantry and fridge, wondering if Gideon would prefer a funfetti toaster waffle or a deluxe cereal combo in the morning. She'd been so sure she wanted to be in this situation with Brandon; she'd stocked up on birth control and everything, which had come in quite handy last night.

This feeling of peace and comfort wouldn't have been there with Brandon, though. She knew that now. Maybe she hadn't gotten naked yet with Gideon, but that had been much more about old habit than wondering how he'd react. She trusted him.

Wow. She really, really did.

He was careful in everything he did and reserved to a fault in his daily life. But not last night. Nosirree. Add *passionate, giving* and *very, very thorough* to his list of better qualities.

Returning to the living room to sandblast the sticky ice cream off the table, she thought about what Nikki had said to her: *Is the fact that Brandon's kind to underdogs a good basis for a relationship?* She'd settled for that in her marriage; she'd been about to do it again with Brandon, desperately seeking a way to feel normal or blessed or something. She'd stopped feeling blessed the moment she'd woken up in the hospital, as if God had abandoned her. She wanted to feel the way she'd felt at fifteen *before* the accident—safe, protected, perfectly average. The truth was she'd never feel the same again. Life had scarred her. Life scarred everybody in one way or another. Ryan, Charlene, Gideon...her mother. Life happened and for better or worse, it left its mark. That didn't mean she was less loved, less protected or less blessed than anyone else.

Gideon would never make her feel "normal." But he made her *feel*.

She hadn't yet told him that she'd attended his lecture and knew how he'd lost his wife. For a man like Gideon, a doctor, it must have been devastating to help his wife die. She wanted to tell him she trusted him completely, that she wanted to be a safe space for all his feelings. He'd fascinated her from the get-go.

Holy cannoli. It had been Gideon all along, hadn't it?

Eden sank to the sofa. Beautiful afflictions— that's what their scars were, the visible ones and the not so visible. Gideon moved more quietly through the world than some others...than Brandon, for example. But he made a difference that was no less profound, being present for Barney and Charlene and Drew and her.

A smile started deep in her belly, beneath the

scars that suddenly, for this one night anyway, seemed more like a tapestry of her life than a hideous disfigurement.

"Night, Malf," she said, rubbing the cat's neck and receiving no response as he slept off his ice cream binge. Rising, Eden put away her cleaning supplies, washed her hands at the kitchen sink and turned off the light as she went back to her bedroom, where not-the-man-of-her-dreams slept, his breathing still deep and steady. As she crawled beneath the sheet again and scooched her body close to his, she let his warmth seep into her. And let her mind accept what the rest of her already knew: she was falling in love with Gideon Bowen.

"This is exactly like *When Harry Met Sally*," Nikki said, sitting across from Eden in the chair she'd pulled up to Eden's desk.

Thanksgiving was one day away, so Nikki was off work, and Holliday House was quiet enough that Eden could have been off. Eden had just finished telling her friend a little bit about the previous night, along with the info that Eden had woken up alone this morning. Alone and somewhat confused, because Gideon had left no note. Not even one of the infamous formal missives that drove her crazy.

"I don't follow you," Eden said in response

to the *WHMS* reference, which happened to be a movie she loved.

"Enemies to friends to lovers to enemies. You just condensed it into a much shorter period of time than Harry and Sally." With her feet on the edge of Eden's immaculate desk, Nikki plucked a piece of jerky from a plastic bag, popped it into her mouth and started chewing. "Do not ever tell my mother I ate dried pig lung." Nikki's parents kept a strict kosher kitchen.

"Why are you eating dried pig lung?"

"Drew says organ meats are higher in vitamins and minerals. Pig lungs are very lean."

"Oh dear God."

Nikki held out the bag. "Do you want to try—"

"No! And for the record, Gideon and I are not becoming enemies again. He always goes to work early. I'm just worried that maybe the night wasn't as…enjoyable for him as it was for me."

"Aw, hon. You did it twice, right? That says something."

"But maybe he regrets it." Which was what was really bothering her.

Nikki shook her head. "'The worst.' That's what Carrie Fisher said to Meg Ryan in *When Harry Met Sally*."

"What?"

"When Sally explains that she and Harry finally did the deed and Sally was all smiles, but Harry regretted doing it and had one foot on the floor when they were in bed together? Marie, who is played by Carrie Fisher, responds, 'The worst.' Because it is. One person glad they had sex when the other person regrets it is the worst. What Sally doesn't know is that Harry is on the phone with Jess, and they're talking about how awkward the night was, too. When everybody gets off the phone, Marie and Jess, who are engaged, promise each other they will never have to be in the dating world again, which is probably one of the biggest perks of getting married."

"What is your point?"

"That Gideon could be regretting the night, but you shouldn't feel bad, because it happened to Meg Ryan, too."

"That's not comforting, Nikki. And now I don't want to see the movie ever again."

"Sorry. The good news is you're over Brandon, because there's something up with that guy." She paused with a piece of pig lung halfway to her mouth. "You are over Brandon, right?"

Eden nodded slowly. "I'm over the idea of him. What do you mean, something's up with him?"

Closing the bag of jerky, Nikki tossed it into her purse, pulled her feet off the desk and looked at her friend seriously. "He acts like what you see is what you get, but I'm not buying it. This past Monday, I walked into the staff room when he was on the phone with someone. He was whispering into his cell, saying, 'Just don't leave. Please just don't leave.' I'm almost positive he was talking to a woman."

"Why didn't you tell me?"

"Because I wasn't positive. I knew how excited you were about your date and didn't want to ruin it. But I put the fear of God into him on your behalf."

"What do you mean?"

Nikki shrugged. "I explained that a relationship with you had to be built on integrity and transparency. And that if he hurt you by being dishonest or due to any other selfish action, this town would run him out on a rail, and I'd be leading the charge. That's all."

"Nik!"

"Well, I don't like him. I don't trust him. He... bugs me. I actually think Gideon is much better for you."

"Really? When did you start thinking that?"

"When he came to the high school to talk to our seniors about careers in medicine."

This was news to Eden. "When did he do that?"

"When I asked him." She reached for her purse. "He's quiet, and he doesn't fawn over everybody. He's like a German shepherd." Standing, she slung the strap of her purse over her shoulder. "I'd better go. I've got to brine an organic turkey. Drew and I are bringing the protein to my parents' Hanukkah party."

"That's a big help." Nikki's mother was French and a fantastic cook. Her daughter's diets drove her crazy. "Are you going to be able to resist the latkes?"

Nikki sighed heavily. "We're going to bring alternative fried food. Drew's making short fries."

"What's that?"

"Turkey balls. He says the testicles are really nutrient rich."

"That's it. Goodbye."

"Bye. I'll call you tomorrow."

After Nikki left, Eden felt restless and angsty. Thoughts of Gideon dominated her mind. She *wanted*—no, that was too pastel a word—she was champing at the bit for a repeat of last night. Nikki's opinion that Gideon was better for her than Brandon had come as a pleasant surprise, but why had it been so damn easy to give up the idea of him? Was she incredibly fickle?

The dream of Brandon had filled her with a giddy, breathless excitement. The reality of Gideon made her feel…calm.

Wow, that was weird. She had felt *calm* with him last night, and the calm inside her had felt indescribably wonderful. She bit her thumbnail. Is that what you were supposed to feel when you met The One?

Where was The One anyway? She checked her cell: no calls, no texts. Not that she'd ever before received a call or text from Gideon, but the day after they'd gone from friendly to...

Crap. Note to self: it's always better to define a relationship before having mad, passionate (it had been), transformative sex.

She drummed her fingernails on the desk. Option one: wait for him to call, text or otherwise contact her. Option two...

Pushing away from the desk, she stood and strode to the museum entrance, so focused on her decision to be boldly proactive that she nearly jumped a foot when the door opened, and Gideon walked in.

Chapter Thirteen

He was dressed in his doctor duds, neat and conservative, and she wanted to rip the clothes off him right there in the foyer, because he was much, much less conservative without them.

"I didn't have time to leave a note this morning," he said without preamble, looking almost as uncalm and unsettled as she felt in this moment.

"Good. You're a terrible note writer."

Beneath his blue dress shirt and navy tie (if this relationship lasted, she was going to buy the man some lighthearted ties), Gideon's chest rose and fell in the same breathless rhythm as hers, as if they'd just ended a quick walk.

He handed her a small brown paper bag with the Holliday Market logo.

"What's this?" Reaching inside, she pulled out a plastic cup of dark berries, yogurt and something that resembled granola, but looked a little more healthful and a whole lot drier. "Yum," she lied to be polite. "Is that plain yogurt?"

"Yes. Cereal in the shape of dinosaurs is not a breakfast food."

"I like dinosaurs. Were you snooping through my cereal, Gideon?"

"It was on top of your refrigerator. You have the eating habits of a preschooler."

"Did you come here to heckle me? Because I'm rather enjoying it."

Gideon's attempt to maintain his serious expression failed, which pleased her enormously. "I came here to ask you if you wanted to have dinner with me."

Delight spread through her. "Why, yes. I would be happy to have dinner with you."

"Good." He swooped in for a quick, hard kiss.

As he walked away, it happened again: that crazy, perfect calm settled inside her like a long-awaited exhale.

Dinner turned out to be a feast of Middle Eastern delicacies, partaken of at his place and prepared by the man himself.

"This is amazing," Eden complimented sincerely as she perused the buffet of goodness in his kitchen shortly after she'd arrived.

"I'm a fan of Yotam Ottolenghi," he said. "I ate in one of his restaurants then bought one of his cookbooks."

"I have no idea what you just said. Am I the only person left on earth who doesn't have a cookbook collection?"

"Quite possibly."

"Well, I don't care. Having you cook for me is hot." Bending forward to examine delectable-looking individual desserts that had a richly coffee-scented icing, she asked, "What do you call these?"

"Dessert." He caught her hand as she reached a finger to the puddle of icing collecting beneath one of the small, muffin-shaped cakes. Bringing her fingers to his lips, he kissed them. "All good things come to those who wait," he murmured, eying her suggestively.

For tonight's date, Eden had changed into a long-sleeved, high-necked, figure-hugging dress in a fire-engine red hue that matched her favorite lipstick. Her hair hung loosely around her shoulders, and she knew her legs were being shown to their best advantage in three-inch, sparkling platform shoes. She'd felt sexy and bold when she'd left her place to walk over here, and Gideon's hot gaze intensified the sensation.

"I hate waiting," she said. "I'm all about immediate gratification."

"Dinner is four courses. What can we do to make the wait easier for you?"

The grin that spread across her face started deep, deep down in her chest. Reaching for Gideon's hand, she asked, "Is there anything that might burn if we leave it too long?"

His grin answered hers. "Only one thing I can think of, and it isn't the food." Turning the oven to Warm, Gideon led Eden out of the kitchen and down the hall toward the bedroom that mirrored hers.

Immediately after work, she had gone to Holliday Fish Market to see Barney. Confusion tended to clear when she talked to him, and she'd been very confused.

"I think I'm falling in love," she'd shared, giving Barney a surprise—a very pleasant one, apparently—when she told him Gideon was the object of her affection.

"Mazel tov, sweetheart!" Barney congratulated her, opening two New York Seltzers to celebrate. "He's a good man, that one. A mensch."

"I know. The thing is," Eden began hesitantly, "I don't know if I feel the right things." She shook her head. "That sounds ridiculous."

"Not so much. Not to someone as old as me." Barney's kind eyes crinkled. "What would 'the right' things be, *maideleh*."

Maideleh. Pretty girl. Barney's endearments warmed her. "You know how you and Charlene call each other *bashert*?" she asked. "How do you know someone is your soul mate? I feel calm when I'm with Gideon. Calm. That can't be right, can it?" She laughed a little incredulously. "The first few days into a romantic relationship, and I'm calm? What did you feel when you were first with Charlene? Excited, right? Fizzy?"

"Fizzy?" Barney repeated, his bushy white brows rising comically. "I don't know about that. Seltzers are fizzy. But they go flat not long after they're opened." Taking a sip of his own drink, he pondered her dilemma. "So you feel calm with Dr. Gideon, and it's unexpected, maybe disappointing. Calm is not what we see between lovers in the movies or on Instagram. What?" he asked as Eden felt her face register her surprise. "You're surprised I know about Instagram? I have an iPhone." Steepling his fingers, he let his gaze grow distant. "For four decades Charlie has sat where you are now. After work, we talk together. She makes tea."

"And you massage her hands."

"Yes. I don't think I've ever felt fizzy during these times." He smiled. "Maybe not calm, either, though. *Whole.* That's the way I'd put it. Being with Charlie has always made me more whole than I am without her. I think she feels the same. Wholeness is greatly underrated."

"She completes you." Eden remembered the impassioned line from *Jerry Maguire*.

Barney considered this. "No. When I'm with my *bashert*, I remember I'm complete already."

And just like that, Eden realized what she'd felt making love with Gideon: complete already.

Walking to the bedroom with him now, she knew tonight would be different. Riskier. And yet, she felt no sense of peril at all.

It was Eden who turned on the lamp on the end table nearest them. Then she walked around the bed and turned the other lamp on as well. Reaching behind her, she unzipped the dress she'd donned and let it slip to the floor. Both her scars and Gideon's expression were on full display.

He took time to appreciate both her body and the meaning of her gesture.

"You're magnificent."

With his eyes on her, she believed it. Standing before him, Eden felt whole—broken and complete and magnificent exactly the way life made her.

As they made love, Eden finally understood the meaning of *bashert*: two souls, each an equal and perfect mate for the other. And finally, finally, she'd found it. With all the lights on.

Chapter Fourteen

Hanukkah in Holliday was busy, noisy and packed with celebrants, both for the practicing Jews living locally and because the magic of the Festival of Lights contagiously spread throughout the town and beyond. From Portland to Salem, folks came to watch the nine-branched, nine-foot-tall menorah light up as they stood in the delicious December cold, sipping hot ciders and cocoas, then heading into the Grange Hall to spin dreidels, make them out of colored clay, watch a puppet show about the Maccabees defeating nasty King Antiochus and, most delicious of all, partake of the dozens of different latkes and *sufganiyot* fried to golden perfection.

A youth choir from Temple Shir Shalom (Song of Peace) in the Rose City serenaded and led sing-alongs of "Ma'oz Tsur," "Judas Maccabaeus," Oh Hanukkah" and "I Have A Little Dreidel."

Shortly after they'd met, Barney had recruited Eden to volunteer on the night of the community party, and she'd loved helping out every year. This year, though, was something special.

Ryan and Olli were already here, Ryan guzzling more than his fair share of cider as they waited for the candle lighting. "Where is he?" Ryan had asked immediately, referencing Brandon, of course.

"I think he's in Washington," she answered lightly. He hadn't called, and, once she'd thought about it, she hadn't expected him to. "Things have changed a bit since I saw you."

"A few days ago?"

"Amazing what can happen in a few days."

"Tell us."

"I'm in love."

Olli whooped and grabbed her for a hug.

"Get down here," Ryan demanded, his hug longer and tighter than Olli's. "Good for you, Ed," he whispered in her ear. When he let her go, he complained, "So when are we going to meet him?"

"You'll meet him tonight."

"I thought you said he's in Washington. He's coming back tonight?"

"No. Not him." She grinned. "I'm in love with the Lord of the Duplex."

"What?" Olli nearly shouted.

"You are one wacky sister," Ryan said, but he was smiling.

"Yes. And I see him coming now, so behave," Eden said, tingling with anticipation as Gideon arrived, accompanying Barney and Charlene. Bundled into her wheelchair, Charlene looked eager to be at the celebration, a small Hanukkiah, the nine-branched menorah, resting on her lap. Barney and Gideon were chatting amiably until Gideon searched the crowd, his gaze finally landing on Eden.

His half-curved smile brought the calm and the fizz. Living next door to him was now the most exciting thing she could imagine. Waiting to see him, wondering what he was doing on the other side of the wall—it was all fantastically, sophomorically, deliciously thrilling. Raising both her arms above her head, she waved to them, ushering the trio over.

"Way to play it cool, Ed," Ryan cracked.

"Oh, shut up," she replied happily.

Gideon and she had not yet gone out to eat together in public or walked down the street together, much less held hands or kissed where someone could see them. She didn't know how he felt about bringing their relationship into the

WENDY WARREN 263

open, how he'd want to play this moment, here in the center of town.

Uncertainty paralyzed her for a few seconds. Then she realized she was standing beneath a giant Hanukkah menorah, the symbol of a great miracle, the reward of people who refused to be erased. She'd spent over half her life minimizing herself and her joy. Now seemed like the perfect night to change.

"Charlene!" she said, bending down to kiss her sweet friend. "Barney, you guys remember Ryan and Olli." She waited while the foursome greeted each other. "Gideon, this is my brother, Ryan, and his fiancé, Ollison. Ry, Olli—I'd like you to meet Gideon. He's my boyfriend." And with that, she tossed her arms around his neck and planted an unmistakably nonplatonic kiss on his lips (no tongue, but you couldn't mistake it).

After the first hesitant moment of surprise, Gideon murmured into her lips, "Hello." Their gazes lingered until he looked away and shook hands with both men.

Ryan was grinning again. "Good to meet you, Gideon. We'll have to find a moment alone tonight to chat, so I can tell you all of Ed's most embarrassing secrets."

"Only if you want me to bring up the time you covered yourself in Mom's olive oil and played 'body builder' in the living room. He was seven," she confided to Olli. "Biceps the size of peas. There are photos."

"You are toast!" Ryan said to her, but he was laughing.

"Uh oh, this could get ugly," Olli interrupted. "Who needs a Hanukkiah?" Beside them, a long table was covered in small Hanukkah menorahs, each with two candles—one in the center and one in the farthest right holder. It was tradition in Holliday to bring your own menorah or to borrow one, so that along with the giant menorah, which was battery operated, the town would be aglow with flickering light.

The boys, Eden and Gideon each took a Hanukkiah. Barney put candles into Charlene's. As the sun set, Rabbi Ari, who traveled in from the coast to officiate each year, stepped up to a microphone and began the ceremony, asking everyone to gather round and for parents to help children carry their lights.

"Eight nights of Hanukkah. It's not just the Jewish response to Santa Claus," Reb Ari said, eliciting a ruffle of laughter, from the parents especially. "So why are we gathered here another year for what amounts to a relatively minor holiday in the Jewish calendar? Maybe you're here for the doughnuts, or to win some Hanukkah *gelt* playing dreidel later. That's all fine. But I doubt any of those reasons will sustain you for eight days, and I hope you will celebrate all eight. In the dark of winter, we need as many candles lit as possible. Not just we Jews, but all of us human beings, whatever our particular winter may be. We need the light, and we need to share it.

"Hanukkah isn't just a chance to say, 'Hey, a miracle once happened.' It's an opportunity to remember that hope and the faith set the stage for miracles. The story goes that a relatively small group of irrepressible rebels refused to be snuffed out. One thimbleful of faith was enough to refuse to die at the hands of a much larger army, and one night's worth of oil for their candelabrum lasted eight days. It's a crazy story, but we tell it every year. Because an act of audacious hope stirs something. Something powerful inside us and maybe outside us, too."

Finding Eden in the crowd, he nodded. That was her cue. "'Scuse me," she said, heart thumping with nerves and excitement as she left their group and made her way to the mic.

Reb Ari addressed the crowd again. "Eden Berman is going to lead us in the lighting of the first-night candle."

Standing next to the rabbi, Eden looked first at her own loves, noting their surprise and their pleasure. Ryan was grinning at her. Gideon looked… well, golly…a little bit awed. A thrill of excitement went through her as she took in the wider group—

so many people, some of here for the fun, some for the food, some for the faith. It didn't matter. For tonight they were together, and they looked happy.

Eden raised her Hanukkiah, so everyone could see it. "For eight days of Hanukkah," she began, "We remember it takes courage to be ourselves and sometimes even more courage to honor the right of the person beside us to do the same. Fear may make us stumble in this effort, but with every light our courage and our hope can grow brighter.

"Tonight, we ask you not to light not your own candle, but the candle of someone next to you. That's important. If you have a child, help them light theirs. It's up to each of us to make sure every candle is lit tonight and that the glow of spirituality illuminates every nook and cranny of darkness. It's only for this one night, but there's no telling how long the glow will last."

Carefully she began to recite the candle blessings she'd been practicing. The rabbi joined her, speaking the Hebrew words. At the end, a collective *"Ah!"* went up as the giant menorah was lit, beginning the first of its eight-night vigil. Eden shivered even though she wasn't cold. She was a sucker for ceremony.

While the Shir Shalom teens sang "Pass the Candle," more lights were kindled. Ryan and Olli lit each other's candles. Barney lit Charlene's, then steadied her stronger hand as she lit his. All around

Eden, menorahs began to flicker, the beauty of it bringing tears to her eyes as she looked for Gideon, wanting to show him herself how to light the *shamash* and then the first Hanukkah candle.

Except that she could no longer locate him anywhere in sea of happy people. Feeling a bit confused—bathroom break that couldn't wait?— Eden made her way to her group. She let Olli light her menorah, but couldn't deny the disappointment over being unable to share this moment with Gideon.

Games and food, including the latke contest, were scheduled to begin. Ryan and Olli were working the dreidel-making station as they had for the past few years. She was supposed to help out where needed and had to get inside.

"Did anyone see where Gideon went?" she asked, but nobody had.

Reminding herself that Gideon was a big boy, his own person, and that he may not have felt as moved as she by the rabbi's words, Eden focused on the celebration as it moved indoors. It was impossible not to catch the sense of universal fun as the party got underway. Everywhere there were children, and they were very quickly smeared with jelly from the doughnuts or color from the clay. As Eden helped out wherever, checking the room periodically to see if Gideon had walked in, she soaked up the joy, easily picturing herself here with her own family someday, feeding her toddler her first latke or watching his eyes grow huge as his daddy spun the dreidel.

Except for Nikki, who was in Portland forcing people to sit at a table with Drew and his turkey testicles, the people Eden loved and trusted the most were here. It was going to be a truly special night.

Gideon stood in the doorway of the Grange Hall, where the Hanukkah party was underway. Good smells, lively decorations and joyful sounds met him, as did the sight of Eden, bending down to hand a young child a doughnut wrapped in waxed paper, then trading a few laughing words with his mother. Earlier, she'd been playing dreidel with a group of tweens.

She belonged here, among people for whom celebrations like this were relished. Gideon found this night nearly intolerable. He wanted to be alone with Eden, not surrounded by...life.

The rabbi's brief service reminded Gideon of how far removed he was from the mainstream. And how damned selfish he had been to allow Eden to believe he could be part of her world. Hope? Courage? Faith in the future and in other people? That wasn't part of him anymore, and he didn't want it to be.

The little girl to whom Eden had given the

doughnut wrapped her arms around Eden's legs, pressing the pastry against her skirt. The child's mother reacted immediately, but Eden laughed, stooping down to offer a hug.

Guilt ate at him. He moved away from the entrance to stand in the shadows outside.

The last time he and Eden were together, she'd told him more about her family's car accident, explained Ryan's injuries as well as her own, and shared that her mother had been self-medicating for years, unable to face the reality that she'd dozed off behind the wheel of the vehicle, causing an accident that changed her children's lives so profoundly. It was a painful story, one with which anyone could empathize, but Gideon had identified the most with the feelings of Eden's mother. The incapacitating shame. The withdrawal from life. The avoidance of any future pain.

The night she'd shared about the accident, he'd ignored the vague awareness that Eden had a right to know more about his life, too—his marriage, Julianne's illness and its aftermath. His and Eden's relationship was new, he'd reasoned with himself; it was casual enough not to require big revelations.

"You're such a bastard," he said to himself, moving away from the building and heading down the street toward home. Nothing about Eden was "casual" when it came to relationships. She connected to people. She *loved*. She belonged. And the likelihood that she would want kids someday appeared pretty damn strong.

He knew what he had to do. He knew. It was going to hurt her, and he'd hate himself for it, but that was a feeling to which he'd grown accustomed. She'd recover. Eden would find someone capable of giving her what she wanted. He saw the way she watched the Gleasons. She wanted what they had; he needed to make it clear that wasn't going to happen with him.

Moreover, he'd watched her while the rabbi was speaking. Her face had glowed brighter than any flame. Tears had gathered in her eyes. He didn't believe in miracles anymore, and he wasn't going to rob her of hers.

There was a darkness that yielded to the light. Then there was a darkness that swallowed the light around it. He couldn't risk doing that to Eden.

He knew she'd attended his lecture at OHSU. How could he miss her when she was in a room? She thought she knew the truth about him, about his marriage and its sad end. She'd probably been waiting for him to bring it up, but, of course, he hadn't. During a lecture, he told only the part of the story he wanted people to hear.

Now it was time for the rest.

Chapter Fifteen

She'd called him three times without receiving a response, asked numerous people if they'd seen him (several had; he'd looked fine—why?) and finally realized Gideon wasn't MIA from the party; he'd gone AWOL.

Eden had lied to her brother about Gideon's disappearance (bad sushi bowl at lunch) and remained to help with the celebration until the other committee members had assured her they were fine and told her to head home. Ry and Olli had left by that time as had Barney and Charlene.

Walking home in deep thought and a healthy measure of anxiety, Eden wasn't all that surprised to see Gideon waiting for her on his porch as she walked up to his door.

Without a word or touch—don't think that wasn't weird—they went into his apartment.

It was warm inside. Eden took off her coat and sat on the couch almost as an act of defiance. *I'm not going anywhere. And, neither are you, so start talking.*

Gideon remained standing.

"So," she opened the conversation for them, "what happened?"

He seemed to understand immediately that she wasn't talking about why he'd left the party. "This time with you was...unexpected. I'm grateful for it."

"Well, damn, Gideon, that's a hell of a way to open the conversation."

"I'm not looking for a relationship with someone. I'm not trying to build a life. And you are. I've been incredibly unfair to you."

"Bad episode of *Bachelor in Paradise*, take one," Eden muttered as his words sunk in. She was being dumped. Mere days after realizing she was in love.

"This is about me," Gideon said. "It's a thousand percent about my inabilities—"

"Will you stop. Okay? Just stop." On one hand, Eden felt as if her head was about to explode. On the other, she felt perfectly in control. "I know it's about you. Because I know we're good together. I'm good for you, and you're good for me, and I don't even want to hear you argue that, because I'm positive it's true." She blew out a hard breath. "Gideon, I know about your wife. I was at OHSU when you gave your lecture. I can't even imagine how difficult it was—"

"Eden—"

"—as a husband, not to mention a doctor, choosing to help your wife—"

"You don't know what you're talking about."

"I won't pretend to understand what you went through, no, but I believe you acted out of immense compassion. I trust you did what you believed was right—"

"*No.* You don't know. You have no idea what you're talking about."

"I know you helped your wife—"

"I did not help my wife!" The words exploded from his lips. "I refused to help her." His anger was so fierce it seemed to be directed everywhere at once. "I wanted her to follow her doctor's orders, take her medicines, try the experimental treatments. When she brought up assisted dying, I took her to a therapist. I didn't help her." Turning partly away from Eden, Gideon scrubbed a hand over his face. "Julianne was ill for most of our marriage. She had a brutal neurological disorder. She knew about it *before* we got married, but the symptoms weren't that evident at first, and she was trying to pretend everything was okay. I think she believed that if she pretended she was well, she would be. So, she didn't say anything about it at first."

"In shock" pretty accurately described how Eden felt on hearing this revelation.

"I loved her. It didn't matter. By the time I realized what was happening, the disease was progressing, and I went into overdrive trying to save her. Julianne's behavior grew increasingly erratic. Excessive spending, some drinking, which didn't help. She had an affair for a while." Gideon stared into the past, rather than at Eden. "She was trying to beat back death, and I guess I was, too, when I dragged her into the latest medical trials. We fought reality with everything in us, and when we couldn't fight anymore, we realized how exhausted we were. She decided on physician-assisted death administered by her husband."

"That wasn't fair to you," Eden said, unsure of whether it was the right thing to say, but certain it was the truth.

"Fair or not," Gideon responded, "I told her I wouldn't have anything to do with it." He sank into a chair, resting his elbows on his knees and pressing his fists to his mouth. After a time, he raised his head. "She called me selfish and unfeeling. I suggested she come to the pediatric wing of the hospital if she wanted to see what dying with dignity looked like. We were both petrified."

The pain on his face was palpable, and Eden felt it in her own heart. He wasn't sparing the details, and she hoped getting it out would be cathartic, because when he was done, she intended to hold him for a very long time.

"If you didn't help her, what happened?"

"She helped herself." Gideon's voice turned flat, monotonal. "She knew she'd lose more and more control of her body, so she ended her life while she still could. Not gently. Not the way medicine could have if I'd been willing to help."

"Gideon." The ache she felt filled his name. Eden rose to go to him, but he shook his head.

"I don't believe in the kinds of miracles you do. I don't want what you want. I never will. I'm not telling you all this so you'll change my mind, or even so you'll understand. I'm telling you so you'll accept that I'm saying goodbye."

Eden lit a candle every night for the eight nights of Hanukkah, keeping her menorah in the window, where menorahs belonged so they could share their light with others. Gideon's apartment remained stubbornly dark during that time. She'd left his apartment the first night of the holiday, and from all appearances he'd moved out the following day.

At no point did he return to the duplex as far as she knew.

"Here we go, people, fried artichoke hearts and fried zucchini." Ollison entered from Eden's kitchen, two platters in his hands. Nikki followed, carrying bowls of dressings for dipping. It was the last night of Hanukkah, food fried in oil still required, but they were all tired of latkes and doughnuts. Ryan was already at the table, tossing a huge salad, and they awaited the arrival of two gourmet pizzas...just 'cause.

Eden believed in miracles, she decided, more than ever before. After leaving Gideon's apartment, she'd cried for three days. Jeremy had sent her home and painfully requested she remain there until she could get through the day without drenching the desk. Nikki had come over every day after school, and her big brother had been, well, quite protective and pretty wonderful.

She'd told Nikki, Ryan and Olli what had gone down with Gideon, without divulging all his business, of course, realizing at some point during the week that in pairing her, however briefly, with Gideon, life had given her a gift—a brand-new view of herself. Nothing could shake her confidence that Gideon, though he may not have loved her, had certainly loved being with her. The wholeness she'd felt with him made her committed never again to hide or disrespect any part of herself. Life was a mashup of the sublime and the ridiculous, the magnificent and the messy. In order to experience one part, you had to be willing to experience it all. The miracle wasn't being magically rescued from suffering; it was knowing your spirit would survive and that you didn't have to do it alone.

She still missed Gideon like crazy—when she wasn't furious with him for refusing to try or filled with grief over what she'd learned about him.

"Thanks for being here, you guys," Eden said, and they all looked at her with similar expressions of understanding.

"You're a goddess," Ollison said.

"True that," Nikki agreed, helping herself to an artichoke heart. "We're all disappointed in Gideon, but the fact is men don't have the emotional resilience that women do. Present company excepted."

"Much appreciated," Ryan quipped. "So, Ed. When will you need help moving?"

"Yeah," said Olli. "I know plenty of unemployed actors who will be happy to help, for a price."

Eden had sent a letter to Gideon's office, informing him of her intention to vacate the apartment. Her chest hurt, thinking about it, but she had to move forward.

"I gave a month's notice." Oh, dang, she was tearing up again. Oh well, couldn't help it. She'd been happy here and lately had enjoyed every moment of living right next door to her lover. When the doorbell rang, she welcomed the opportunity to escape the concerned glances traveling around the table. "That's the pizza. I'll get it."

Wiping her eyes as she headed for the door, Eden opened it, expecting two extra thick crust kitchen-sink pies, but finding Gideon instead.

He was wearing the Irish fisherman's sweater she loved on him. His hair was less neat than usual, his expression as intense as ever.

"Hello," she said.

"Happy Hanukkah."

"It's the last night," she said, apropos of nothing.

"I know." He looked a little…nervous. "I saw the candles through the window, and I… I'm sorry if I'm interrupting. May I come in?"

She stepped back, and Gideon entered, stopping short when he saw Ryan, Ollison and Nikki staring at him. "We thought you were pizza," Nikki said, clearly sounding displeased with him. Ryan backed his chair away from the table and wheeled it forward. Ollison joined him. Her army of supporters.

Gideon acknowledged them all, looking uncomfortable but resigned that he was going to have to say whatever he'd come to say in front of them. He turned to her. "You sent me a month's notice."

She nodded. "That's right. I'm moving."

"I deserve that. I do. I deserve to have to watch you walk out of this apartment and not look back."

Gideon looked tired, as if he'd been awake for several days. "Please don't," he said. "Don't leave."

A million different thoughts crowded her mind.

"I thought I could tell you this privately, but…" He shook his head. "I guess it doesn't matter. The only thing that matters is I can't lose you. And I don't really deserve a second chance—I probably didn't deserve a first one—but I've been trying to forget how it feels to hold you, and it's not possible. I'm never going to be able to forget that, because when you're in my arms, this crazy, broken world begins to make sense.

"I thought there was only so much pain a person could hold and that I'd reached my limit." Gideon's storm-gray eyes had never looked at her more openly. "I know how it feels to fail someone you love. I don't ever want to do that to you."

"You will, though," Eden assured him in a whisper, which was all she could manage.

"Definitely," Ryan said behind her, with accompanying affirmative murmurs from the rest of the crew. "Sorry," Ry apologized when Eden and Gideon looked over.

Smiling ruefully at the peanut gallery, Gideon lowered his head. Taking her hands, he held them gently. This time when he looked up to meet Eden's eyes, his whole heart was on display. "I'm terrified to hurt you and too selfish to walk away. I have a lot of scars."

"Turns out I'm not afraid of scars."

Hope and gratitude filled the face she had come to think of as just perfect. "Eden Berman, I haven't even begun to feel everything I'm willing to feel with you. If you'll have me. If you'll put up with a stumbling, cranky doctor who thought 'First do no harm' was more important than 'Physician, heal thyself—'" raising her hands to his lips, he kissed them. "—there's no limit. No limit to how happy we can make this life. I get that now. And the rest we can face together. Will you give me another chance to get this right?"

Eden pulled her hands from his, then wound her arms around Gideon's neck. "Way more than one chance." She moved as close as she could get. "I think we should give each other as many chances as it takes."

Gideon wrapped her in a hug that felt safer than anything she'd felt before, and their lips met. She would never, ever get enough of his lips. Or of the way he could seem strong and vulnerable, absolutely confident and honestly scared at the same time. Holding his hand, she could walk any path put in front of them.

"Just one thing," she muttered against his lips.

"Hmm?"

"I'm not giving up my dinosaur cereals. There's a toy dinosaur in every box."

"I want the T. rex."

She grinned against him. "We'll talk."

"Man, they're weird," she heard Ryan say.

"Yeah," Nikki agreed, a teary smile in her voice.

Gideon pulled Eden tighter, and as they kissed, the flames of hope kindled and glowed, making the shadows of the past recede and lighting the path for the future.

* * * * *

*Look for Nikki's story,
the next installment of Wendy Warren's
new miniseries,
Holliday, Oregon
Coming soon to Harlequin Special Edition.*

#2881 THEIR NEW YEAR'S BEGINNING
The Fortunes of Texas: The Wedding Gift • by Michelle Major

Brian Fortune doesn't think he will ever find the woman he kissed at his brother's New Year's wedding. So when the search for the provenance of a mysterious gift leads him into a local antique store a few days later, he's stunned to find Emmaline Lewis, proprietor—and mystery kisser! Brian has never been the type to commit, but suddenly he knows he'll do anything to stay at Emmaline's side—for good.

#2882 HER HOMETOWN MAN
Sutton's Place • by Shannon Stacey

Summoned home by her mother and sisters, novelist Gwen Sutton has made it clear—she's not staying. She's returning to her quiet life as soon as the family brewery is up and running. But when Case Danforth offers his help, it's clear there's more than just beer brewing! Time is short for Case to convince Gwen that a home with him is where her heart is.

#2883 THE RANCHER'S BABY SURPRISE
Texas Cowboys & K-9s • by Sasha Summers

Former soldier John Mitchell has come home after being discharged and asks to stay with his best friend, Natalie. They're both in for a shock when a precious baby girl is left on Natalie's doorstep—and John is the father! Now John needs Natalie's help more than ever. But Natalie has been in love with John forever. How can she help him find his way to being a family man if she's not part of that family?

#2884 THE CHARMING CHECKLIST
Charming, Texas • by Heatherly Bell

Max Del Toro persuaded his friend Ava Long to play matchmaker in exchange for posing as her boyfriend for one night. He even gave her a list of must haves for his future wife. Except now he can't stop thinking about Ava—who doesn't check a single item on his list!

#2885 HIS LOST AND FOUND FAMILY
Sierra's Web • by Tara Taylor Quinn

Learning he's guardian to his orphaned niece sends architect Michael O'Connell's life into a tailspin. He's floored by the responsibility, so when Mariah Anderson agrees to pitch in at home, Michael thinks she's heaven-sent. He's shocked at the depth of his own connection to Mariah and opens his heart to her in ways he never imagined. But can an instant family turn into a forever one?

#2886 A CHEF'S KISS
Small Town Secrets • by Nina Crespo

Small-town chef Philippa Gayle's onetime rival-turned-lover Dominic Crawford upended her life. But when she's forced together with the celebrity cook on a project that could change her life, there's no denying that the flames that were lit years ago were only banked, not extinguished. Can Philippa trust Dominic enough to let him in...or are they just cooking up another heartbreak?

*Brian Fortune doesn't think he will ever find the
woman he kissed at his brother's New Year's wedding.
So when the search for the provenance of a mysterious
gift leads him into a local antique store a few days
later, he's stunned to find Emmaline Lewis, proprietor—
and mystery kisser! Brian has never been the type to
commit—but suddenly he knows he'll do anything to
stay at Emmaline's side—for good...*

*Read on for a sneak peek of the first book in the
The Fortunes of Texas: The Wedding Gift continuity,
Their New Year's Beginning,
by USA TODAY bestselling author Michelle Major!*

"I'd like to take you out on a proper date then."

"Okay." Color bloomed in her cheeks. "That would be
nice." He leaned in, but she held up a finger. "You should
know that since Kirby and the gang outed my pregnancy
at the coffee shop, I'm not going to hide it anymore." She
pressed a hand to her belly. "I'm wearing a baggy shirt
tonight because it seemed easier than fielding questions
from the boys, but if we go out, there will be questions.
And comments."

"I don't care about what anyone else thinks," he
assured her and then kissed her gently. "This is about you
and me."

Those must have been the right words, because Emmaline wound her arms around his neck and drew closer. "I'm glad," she said, but before he could kiss her again, she yawned once more.

"I'll walk you to your car."

She mock pouted but didn't argue. "I'm definitely not as fun as I used to be," she told him as he picked up the bags with the leftover supplies to carry for her. "Actually I'm not sure I was ever that fun."

"As far as I'm concerned, you're the best."

After another lingering kiss, Emmaline climbed into her car and drove away. Brian watched her taillights until they disappeared around a bend. The night sky overhead was once again filled with stars, and he breathed in the fresh Texas air. He needed to stay in the moment and remember his reason for being in town and how long he planned to stay. He knew better than to examine the feeling of contentment coursing through him.

One thing he knew for certain was that it couldn't last.

Don't miss
Their New Year's Beginning *by Michelle Major,*
available January 2022 wherever
Harlequin Special Edition books and ebooks are sold.

Harlequin.com

Get 4 FREE REWARDS!

We'll send you 2 FREE Books plus 2 FREE Mystery Gifts.

Harlequin Special Edition books relate to finding comfort and strength in the support of loved ones and enjoying the journey no matter what life throws your way.

FREE Value Over **$20**

The corridor ended, and he stood in front of another set of towering doors. Kenan briefly hesitated, then grasped the handle, opened the doors and slipped through to the balcony beyond. The cool April night air washed over him. The calendar proclaimed spring had arrived, but winter hadn't yet released its grasp over Boston, especially at night. But he welcomed the chilled breeze over his face, let it seep beneath the confines of his tuxedo to the hot skin below. Hoped it could cool the embers of his temper...the still-burning coals of his hurt.

"For someone who is known as the playboy of Boston society, you sure will ditch a party in a hot second." Slim arms slid around him, and he closed his eyes in pain and pleasure as the petite, softly curved body pressed to his back. "All I had to do was follow the trail of longing glances from the women in the hall to figure out where you'd gone."

He snorted. "Do you lie to your mama with that mouth? There was hardly anyone out there."

"Fine," Eve huffed. "So I didn't go with the others and watched all of that go down with your parents and brother. I waited until you left the ballroom and went after you."

"Why?" he rasped.

He felt rather than witnessed her shrug. The same with the small kiss she pressed to the middle of his shoulder blades. He locked his muscles, forcing his head not to fall back. Ordering his throat to imprison the moan scrabbling up from his chest. Commanding his dick to stand down.

"Because you needed me," she said.

So simple. So goddamn true.

He did need her. Her friendship. Her body.

Her heart.

But since he could only have one of those, he'd take it. With a woman like her—generous, sweet, beautiful of body and spirit—even part of her was preferable to none of her. And if he dared to profess his true feelings, that was exactly what he would be left with. None of her. Their friendship would be ruined, and she was too important to him to risk losing her.

Carefully, he turned and wrapped her in his embrace, shielding her from the night air. Convincing himself if this was all he could have of her—even if it meant Gavin would have all of her—then he would be okay, he murmured, "You're really going to have to remove 'rescue best friend' off your résumé. For one, it's beginning to get too time-consuming. And two, the cape clashes with your gown."

She chuckled against his chest, tipping her head back to smile up at him. He curled his fingers against her spine, but that didn't prevent the ache to trace that sensual bottom curve.

"Where would be the fun in that? You're stuck with me, Kenan. And I'm stuck with you. Friends forever."

Friends.

The sweet sting of that knife buried between his ribs.

"Always, sweetheart."

Don't miss what happens next in
The Perfect Fake Date *by Naima Simone,*
the next book in the Billionaires of Boston series!

Available January 2022 wherever
Harlequin Desire books and ebooks are sold.

Harlequin.com